run for your life

run for your life

Marilyn Levy

Houghton Mifflin Company
Boston 1996

For information about this and other Houghton Mifflin
trade and reference books and multimedia products,
visit The Bookstore at Houghton Mifflin on the
World Wide Web at http://www.hmco.com/trade/.

Manufactured in the United States of America
Book design by Celia Chetham
The text of this book is set in 12.5 pt. Joanna

BP   10   9   8   7   6   5   4   3   2   1

Library of Congress Cataloging-in-Publication Data
Levy, Marilyn.
Run for your life / Marilyn Levy.
p.   cm.
Summary: While living in a housing project in Oakland,
California, thirteen-year-old Kisha joins a track team
which helps her discover that she can be a winner.
ISBN 0-395-74520-9
[1. Inner cities — Fiction.   2. Track and field — Fiction.
3. Afro-Americans — Fiction.]   I. Title
PZ7.L58325Ru   1996
[Fic] — dc20   95-24379   CIP   AC

For Darrell Hampton
and the Acorn Track Team.

Against all odds, you've shown everyone
what it takes to be real winners.

1

Some people think 13 is an unlucky number. Me — I used to think it was magical. I couldn't wait to be a teenager. But my birthday came and went, and nothing happened. I didn't look different. I didn't feel different, either. That was April — just four months ago. Then suddenly, like overnight, my jeans were too short. For a minute I thought I'd put on my brother Tyrone's by mistake. Then I realized this was it. I was finally turning into a real teenager. I was ready for the magic to begin.

I waited and waited.

But again, nothing happened.

Sometimes I wish it was the end of summer vacation, instead of the beginning of July. Not that I want to go back to school, or anything. But sometimes I get tired of summer, and sometimes it gets a little difficult around the house. Noisy. Too noisy. I don't really mind noise.

It's just that there's noise and there's noise. Music is good noise. TV is good noise, unless Tyrone is watching the news. Tyrone is a news freak, and he's only nine years old. If we had cable, I'm sure he'd be plugged in to CNN all day.

Tyrone is not like other kids. He hates sports. He doesn't even like to watch football games on television. But my dad does. That's about all he ever watches besides cop shows. My mom watches soaps when my dad's not watching his shows. Sometimes they fight about whether she gets to watch her soap, or he gets to watch the five hundredth rerun of *NYPD Blue*. They always wind up watching the cop show. At least my dad does. My mom goes next door to her girlfriend's.

I don't watch TV all that much. Maybe talk shows once in a while. Mainly, I like to listen to music and hang out with my friend Natonia, who lives at the other end of the project. It's not that I have anything against TV. It's just that I like to avoid fighting. Or listening to fights. Natonia says I'm a wussy. "No one would ever believe you grew up in the projects, girl," she always says to me. "You don't know nothing about nothing."

Well, I might not know as much as she does, but I know a lot more than she thinks I do. I just don't say it.

I know, for example, that right now my parents are in the kitchen arguing. And this is the kind of noise that really bugs me. Even though my bedroom door is closed and I have my earphones plugged into my ears, I know they're fighting. And I know what they're fighting about, too. Money. Actually, the lack of it. That's *the* big issue here. My mom wants to get a job, but my dad says it's no use working for minimum wage because then we can't get welfare. After paying taxes, we'd wind up with less than we have now.

Personally, I wish my dad could get another job. He's been out of work for two years, which means he can't collect unemployment anymore. Of course, just to complicate things, my mom thought she was pregnant last month. My dad about had a fit, even though he was at least as responsible as she was. Luckily, she wasn't pregnant, so everything worked out okay. We couldn't fit one more person into this apartment. Not even a baby. Tyrone and I have to share a room as it is. Basically, I guess that's not so bad, but sometimes I need to have private conversations with my friends, and Ty's in there doing what he needs to do. Besides that he has allergies, or something, and he snores. He also looks at my hair and rolls his eyes.

That's the one thing that didn't change about me this summer, the one thing I really, really wish would change. My hair. My mom's hair is almost straight. And it's not because she does anything to it, either. It's just naturally that way. Sort of wavy, but not frizzy like mine. Natonia wears her hair in corn rows, and it looks cool, but I can't get mine to grow long enough to do that. I've tried, but it looks stupid. I end up with these two-inch braids sticking up all over my head. I wouldn't be caught dead walking outside looking like that. I condition my hair every time I wash it, but it's just impossible. Which is why I wear a baseball cap all the time.

I've seen old pictures of some of my aunts wearing African dashikis. They have huge Afros sticking out about five inches from their heads. I could probably do something like that, but my mom thinks that kind of look is nasty.

Some of the people around Walt Whitman, our housing project, still wear their hair in sort of a modified Afro style. But not many people have the kind of mean-looking hair I do.

And most people around here don't dress in African dashikis anymore. They dress just like everyone else. Some people even wear expensive black leather jackets, with lots of studs, and cowboy boots. Some people have rings with diamonds as big as a rock. I don't know any of those people. I mean, I know them, but I don't *know* them. I know them by name and by reputation. I don't hang out with them, but I know how they get all the money to buy their fancy clothes.

My mom doesn't like me to go over to Natonia's house. Her uncles have a reputation. Natonia doesn't ever talk about it. But I know. She doesn't think I know, but I know. Everyone knows. Even Tyrone. I think that's why Tyrone watches the news all the time. He doesn't like to go outside. Too much going on out there. Especially in this neighborhood.

I learned a long time ago that those popping sounds we hear are not cars backfiring, the way my mom used to pretend. I made a big mistake about five years ago, when I was still young and naive, and I said that once in front of Natonia. She about cracked up. "Girl," she said, "next time you hear a car backfiring like that, fall to the floor so it won't run you over."

I think that's another reason Tyrone watches TV. To see if any of those "cars" killed anyone we know. So far we've been lucky.

My mom says Walt Whitman wasn't always such a mess. She's lived in Oakland all her life. Right in this very housing project. In a different apartment, of course, but one that looked just like this one. Her mother came here from Tennessee, married my grandpa, I think, and had about twenty kids. One of which was my mom. They were too poor to travel any-place, so my mom never even left Oakland, except to go to San Francisco when she got married to my father.

5

She says that the project was designed to look nice, so people would enjoy living here. No high-rise ghettoes, she said. Two- and three-story buildings with little courtyards. Every courtyard had a barbecue and picnic benches. There were flowers. Now there's concrete pretty much everyplace. Things got kind of out of hand the last few years, I guess. "You know how it is," my mom always says. "There are people living here who have no pride in themselves. No pride in the way they make their living or in the way they live."

I don't know. Maybe that's true. Maybe not. Maybe it's so nasty around here because so many people just don't have anything to call their own and don't see much chance of getting it in the future, either.

My mom's friend, Deandra, lives next door and works in the office that runs the housing project. She says you'd never believe the way some people treat their apartments. When they leave, they tear the curtains off the windows, destroy the kitchen cabinets, make a total mess. I think that's so disgusting. My mom thinks it's sick. Just 'cause you're poor, you don't have to live like a pig, she says. And I agree with her.

Of course, she avoids the leather crowd as much as she avoids the slobs, but if I had to choose between them, I guess I'd have to choose the drug pushers. At least they *look* great, even though they can be really mean to you if you get in their way.

They tried to recruit Tyrone, once. He didn't tell me. As far as I know, he didn't tell anyone. Natonia told me. One of her uncles told her. Maybe it was even one of her uncles who actually did the recruiting. Or tried to.

They like to get nine- and ten-year-olds — boys mostly. The boys let them know if there's anyone suspicious coming into the project — like the police. Not that the police spend much time here, actually. Not that I know of, anyway. You call them, and they don't show up for hours. But the drug pushers show up. Because they can escape down the walkways, and no one can find them. I guess that's why they like Whitman so much.

My mom's friend, Deandra, says the pushers are the only tenants who pay their rent on time — and in cash. So the people who run the project don't want to kick them out. Well, I can see their point, I guess, but sometimes that doesn't make it a very pleasant place to live. Especially, if you live where Natonia does. Near Filbert Street where the crack pushers hang out, and the junkies who are their customers. Filbert's the worst. Cocaine and marijuana are sold on the other streets, and that's bad enough, but Filbert's *Filbert,* and everybody knows how rough it can get.

My mom always told me not to hang around Filbert, even though it looks just like any other street. Maybe a little wider. She says it's too dangerous. I didn't take her seriously, at first. My mom thinks everything's dangerous. She walked me to school until I was in third grade. She'd have gone on walking me till I graduated from high school if I'd let her. But knowing what I know now, I think my mom's probably right. Filbert *is* dangerous. I don't make a big deal out of it, but I go out of my way to avoid it.

Natonia walks anywhere she wants to. She sees a drug deal going down, and she just laughs. Four or five years ago, I didn't even know what she meant by "deals." I didn't want to ask her outright 'cause I knew she'd just crack up again, but I kept my ears open, and I finally pieced it all together.

Natonia's lucky. She grew up naturally smart. I'm not sure how she knows everything, but she just does.

2

I figured if I took off my shoes and whizzed past the kitchen they wouldn't hear me or see me, and I could get out the door without being grilled. So I looked straight ahead, didn't even say good-bye to Tyrone, and raced out. Once I got to the sidewalk I realized they wouldn't have heard me if I'd have come through wearing combat boots. They were mad. It was kind of scary. Usually, they waited to have their real bad fights till they got to their bedroom, but this time they were going at it in the kitchen, and they didn't care who heard them. Poor Ty. Even with the TV turned way up, he could still hear them. Hell, I was outside and *I* could still hear them.

The heat was beginning to get to me, too. It had been building up for two weeks. Every day was hotter and hotter. I couldn't remember it ever being so hot. It was getting on my nerves. I felt like jumping into a nice big swimming pool, but I didn't know where to find one. And to make matters worse, everything around me was totally dried up. Even the pavement looked gray and dusty. Flowers were here and there in pots on people's stoops, but they'd pretty much dried up, too.

I noticed a fan blowing in someone's kitchen window as I passed. A fat lady was standing in front of it, mopping up her face and neck. Bet she wished she had air conditioning.

I pulled my shirt away from my body, then I took my Oakland A's cap off and shook it out. If I lived in a real house like they have on TV, with lots of rooms and a yard in front, I'd be sitting in my room right now with the air conditioner going full blast.

As I rounded the corner, I could see Natonia sitting on the stoop in front of her grandmother's apartment. She was just sitting there, her skinny shoulders slumped into a "U," staring off into space. I waved. She didn't see me at first. But as soon as she spotted me, she jumped up, almost tripping over her long legs. That's the thing about Natonia. Her legs look like they start at her shoulders and work their way down to the floor, like two narrow poles. Despite my recent growth spurt, she still stands over a head taller than me.

"Hot," I said, sitting down on the step.

"You ain't kidding," Natonia said, slumping down next to me.

"Whatcha doing?"

"Nothing."

"Me neither."

"Hot."

"Yeah."

"Wanna get ice cream?"

"Sure."

"You got some money?"

"No. You?"

"You kidding?"

"Maybe we could go into your place and get a cold drink of water instead."

"Forget about the drink," Natonia said, hauling herself up from the stoop again. "Come on. There's always lots of cans down by the Johnson's place."

"What good's that gonna do us?"

"Girl, sometimes I wonder about you," Natonia said. She was obviously disgusted with me.

"Oh," I said. "I get it."

Natonia started walking toward the Johnson's place. I followed her, hoping we wouldn't have to go inside their apartment to get the cans because I didn't think I wanted to do that even for a chocolate pecan ice cream cone. Talk about people who had no pride. The Johnsons were in a category all by themselves.

We were almost in front of their apartment when we heard screaming and shouting, like someone was getting killed, or something. I was a little nervous, but Natonia didn't pay any attention. She was used to it, I guess. I walked in back of her, sort of hunkered down — just in case.

"Look at this," she said, kicking a cardboard box.

The box was overflowing with beer cans.

"It's all sitting here just waiting for us," she said triumphantly, as she bent over and peered in.

I stood there watching her.

"What you doing, just standing there? I can't carry all these cans by myself."

She reached into the garbage bin next to the cardboard box and pulled out two bags filled with some vile smelling stuff. Then she turned them upside down into the bin and started filling one of the bags with the empty beer cans.

My stomach was turning around and around, heading for my throat. I could feel my breakfast coming up fast, but I wasn't going to show Natonia what a wussy I was this time. I reached for the second bag and began filling it with the rest of the cans. Natonia looked over at me and smiled. I started packing the cans in faster.

When we had filled both bags, Natonia started walking off toward Filbert Street.

"Where we going?" I asked as nonchalantly as I could.

"To the store. Where'd you think?"

"That's what I thought," I said. "Just wanted to make sure."

"I think we're gonna get enough cash for these cans to buy us two scoops apiece," she said as she mentally calculated how many cans we had in each bag.

Natonia was so smart.

Suddenly, I stopped walking.

"Which store we going to?" I asked.

"The grocery store."

"You mean the supermarket?"

"Why should we go all the way down to the supermarket? The grocery store's only two blocks away."

"We could probably get more money for the cans at the supermarket," I said, though I had no idea if this was true.

"You get the same refund everyplace," Natonia said. "No reason to walk the extra three blocks, especially in this heat."

"But I — "

"Yeah?"

"It's just that I — "

"You what?"

"Nothing."

"What?"

"I don't like walking on Filbert Street, is all."

Natonia gave me her most disgusted look.

"I mean I *will* walk on Filbert. It's just that I don't really like to," I added quickly.

"Uh huh," Natonia said, crossing over to Filbert.

"Wait up," I called, running after her.

There were three guys standing in the middle of the block, talking and laughing. A fancy car pulled up, and one of the guys walked over to the driver's side and handed the driver a small package. The driver handed him an envelope, and he stuffed it in his pocket. Then the fancy car drove off, and the guy slapped the other guys' hands and they all laughed real loud.

"You see that?" I asked Natonia.

"Don't point," Natonia whispered nervously. "Don't ever point."

"Forgot," I said.

"You can't afford to forget. They'd just as soon kill you, as look at you," Natonia warned. "The only people who point at them are pointing them out to someone who has no business knowing who they are and what they're doing."

She smiled at the guys as we passed by them and

flashed a "V," which was pretty difficult because she was still holding the bag of cans. That was a signal to let them know we know, but it's okay that we know 'cause we would never tell anyone we know. And now that they know we won't, we won't have any trouble with them when we pass by.

We walked to the end of the block.

"Drugs, huh?" I whispered.

"What do you think? This is Filbert Street, girl. There's only one reason why a shiny new BMW pulls up to three guys standing in their regular spot, and it's not to get directions, believe me."

"Makes me sick, these rich guys coming down here to score. How come the pushers don't hang around *their* neighborhoods, instead of taking up space on our street corners?"

Natonia laughed. "How long you think a black guy standing around their neighborhood would last?"

"That makes me sick, too."

"You live *there,* you got lots of choices. You live *here,* you got two choices — earning minimum wage at McDonald's or maximum wage selling drugs. Either way, you ain't gonna live too long. People shoot you up here because you got what they need. Or they stick you up at McDonald's to get the money to pay for it. And the thing is — people could be shooting each other up for five minutes around here, and the cops would never come. So whatever you do, you're dead meat."

"I know that," I said as I kicked open the door of the grocery store.

We dumped the cans on the counter. Mr. Abrakus, the owner, a gray-haired white man with tired blue eyes, counted them, multiplied in his head, opened the cash register, and handed us two dollars and twenty cents.

"Thanks," I said.

"Hold it," Natonia said. "You owe us fifty cents more."

"You accusing me of trying to short you?" Mr. Abrakus asked, angrily.

I was getting real nervous.

"Yeah," Natonia said defiantly.

"You can't multiply that fast," he said.

"Gimme the cans back," Natonia demanded.

"I'm doing you a favor," Mr. Abrakus said.

"You ain't doing anybody any favors," Natonia said.

I started pulling on her sleeve. "Let's get out of here," I whispered. I didn't want any trouble. I'd been in the store a few times before with my mom. She'd run in when she had to get a few things and didn't have time to stop at the supermarket. But she didn't like Mr. Abrakus and tried to avoid coming here. I didn't like him much either. He scared me.

To my surprise, Natonia grabbed a bag of cans, turned around and headed for the door. I almost ran to open it for her. I wanted to get out of there as fast as I could, but somehow Mr. Abrakus got to the door ahead of me.

"Gimme the bag," he demanded. "I paid for those cans."

"You paid for some of them," Natonia said, standing her ground.

I started to sweat. My mouth felt dry.

Natonia and Mr. Abrakus stood staring at each other for a long time.

I wasn't sure what was going to happen next. I kept inching closer to the door, but I wasn't sure why. I couldn't get out anyway. Mr. Abrakus was blocking it.

Finally, Mr. Abrakus reached into his pocket and pulled out some change. Angrily, he tossed it at Natonia.

"Don't come back," he said, walking away from the door.

"Thanks," I said. My head was reeling. It felt like all the blood had drained out of it. I was afraid I was going to faint.

"Up yours," Natonia said. She dropped the bag of cans on the floor, gave Mr. Abrakus the finger, and walked out the door.

"Let's go," she said to me without skipping a beat, like it didn't even faze her.

I still had a little trouble breathing, but I walked along beside her, relieved to be outside again.

"Told you we'd have enough for double scoops," Natonia said.

"How did you do that?" I asked.

"Do what?"

"The math. How'd you do the math so fast?"

"Didn't."

"Then how'd you know Mr. Abrakus was short-changing us?"

"Instinct," she said, shrugging her shoulders.

3

We were back at Natonia's, sitting on her stoop again, and I was enjoying every bit of that ice cream cone. Ice cream had never, ever tasted so good.

"Ummmmm," I cooed as I popped the last bite into my mouth.

"Oooooh, look at that," Natonia said.

"What?" I mumbled.

"Look at him," Natonia said, pointing to a guy walking toward us.

"I thought you said not to point."

"You can point at him," Natonia said. "He's nobody."

"Looks like somebody to me. He's dressed nice."

"Too nice," Natonia said, looking him over carefully. "Expensive, but not sharp, if you know what I mean."

"I know what you mean."

"Now you do," Natonia said. She laughed good-naturedly. "I've never seen him around here before," she said, narrowing her eyes.

"Me neither."

"He's dressed too nice for a cop. But not nice enough for a drug pusher. And he looks too straight to be a junkie. On the other hand, you can't always tell."

By now the guy is almost up to us, and I can see Natonia's still trying to figure out what his business is here.

He stops and smiles. I smile back. Natonia cocks her head to the side and says almost meanly, "You looking for somebody?"

"Sure am," the guy says, all enthusiastically, like some kind of cheerleader, or something. But he seemed nice to me, anyway.

"You looking for my uncles?" Natonia says, narrowing her eyes.

"Nope," the guy says. "I'm looking for you."

Natonia jumps up, her body poised for running. "You a social worker?"

"I'm the new director of the community center," the guy says pointing to the ugly gray cinder-block building down the street, which hadn't been used for anything but graffiti and target practice for the past year and a half. The windows are boarded up because they've been broken so many times the management refuses to replace them anymore.

"Yeah?" Natonia says, relaxing slightly.

"Yeah," the guy says, holding out his hand. "I'm Darren Hayes."

Natonia looks at his hand, but she doesn't take it.

"I'm Kisha Clark," I say holding out my hand.

He pumps it hard.

"How come you're looking for me?" Natonia asks, still suspicious of him.

"I'm looking for girls."

"You and every other guy around here," Natonia says sarcastically.

Darren laughs. He's got a dimple running down the left side of his cheek, and when he laughs he looks really cute. Almost babyish, even though he must be about twenty-five or twenty-six. A big guy, too. Looks to me like he was probably a football player, or something like that, 'cause his neck is so thick.

I like the way he looks. Nice hair, clipped real short, big full lips. And real chocolate skin, like my dad's. My mom and I are much lighter, but we always say we're attracted to dark-skinned men. Of course, I don't do anything but look, but lots of girls my age do a lot more than that.

"How come you're looking for girls?" Natonia asks.

21

"I'm gonna start a track team," Darren announces.

My heart drops. "I can't run," I mumble.

"You got two good legs. You can run," Darren says.

"Why should we?" Natonia asks.

"Because it's good for you. It's healthy. It's fun."

"Sure," Natonia says.

"It is," Darren says.

He turns to me and gives me the once-over. I feel like melting into the ground. The palms of my hands are hot and moist, and I'm embarrassed because I wonder if they felt that way when I shook hands with Darren.

"I can tell just by looking at you, you'd make a terrific runner," he says to me.

I want to be cool. I can feel Natonia staring at me. I know Darren is. I can't stand it.

"If you work hard, you can be a winner," Darren says.

"Who are you to promise that?" Natonia asks, belligerently.

Before Darren can answer, Natonia turns around and walks into her apartment building.

I'm embarrassed. I don't know what to say. I can see that he's embarrassed, too. I'd like to be a winner. I'm willing to work hard, but I've never been much of an athlete. In fact, my dad always says I have two left feet. I don't know. Maybe I do. Maybe I do around him.

"So," Darren says to me. "Give it a try?"

"Me?"

"Yeah."

"I don't know."

"Why not? What have you got to lose?"

"I'm not sure. I don't want to look stupid."

"I can understand that," Darren says softly, and somehow I know he can.

"Maybe I will give it a try," I say, as Natonia slams out of the house.

"I'm already a winner," she says, holding out a bunch of medals to Darren. "These are for track."

"Then I need you on my team," Darren says. "Be at the community center tomorrow morning at eight-thirty. Both of you."

He walked away quickly.

"Where'd you get those?" I asked Natonia when he was gone. "You steal them?"

"They're my mother's," Natonia answered as she stuffed the medals into her pocket. "She left them here."

"I didn't know your mother was a runner," I said, hoping Natonia would tell me something about this mother of hers who was someone I'd never met. Far as I knew no one else around the project had met her either. Word is she arrived with Natonia when Natonia was a baby, then she disappeared the next day. Only thing Natonia ever said about her was that she had some big job in San Francisco, and she had no time to take care of her, so she had left her with her grandmother.

Once I made a big, big mistake. I asked Natonia how come her mother never came to visit her. Not even on Christmas or her birthday.

"Because," she said. And that was it. And I knew the subject was closed. She never mentioned her mother again until now.

"Lots of things you don't know about my mother," Natonia said.

"Like what?" I asked, softly.

"If I wanted you to know, I'd tell you," Natonia said sharply.

"I gotta go," I said to Natonia.

I walked away without even looking at her. Sometimes she made me so mad. First she says there's lots of things I don't know about her mother. Like she's opening the door for me to ask her, and when I do, she slams the door right in my face. That is so frustrating. Either she ought to tell me, or she ought to keep her mouth shut. It's like she can't even make up her own mind whether she wants to talk about her mother, or not.

"Damn," I said to myself.

4

I found an empty can and kicked it all the way home. I kind of liked the way it sounded, bouncing on the sidewalk.

Just before I got to my apartment house, I stepped on the can. Squash. Then I picked it up in case Natonia and I decided to go get ice cream again. If we were still friends, that is. Natonia is a little moody. Occasionally, I'd give her a call and tell her I was coming over, and she'd tell me she was busy. Just like that. Busy. She never tells me what she's so busy doing, of course. And I never ask. But sometimes she can be busy for two whole days. Then she'll call me like nothing in the world is the matter. I don't think that's any way to treat your best friend, but Natonia's not the type to tell anyone what's on her mind, not even me.

Which is why I left her apartment house. If I had told

her what I really wanted to tell her, she'd have been mad, mad, mad. And she probably would never speak to me again. Even though I was mad at her, she was still my best friend, and I didn't want to take any chances.

I stood outside the apartment for a minute before I opened the door. All I could hear was the TV on as usual, so I went in.

I glanced at the kitchen. It was empty. The only sound coming from there was the groan of the old refrigerator.

"You're going to burn your eyes out watching that thing," I said to Ty as I walked into the living room.

"The whole world's at war," Ty said, rolling over on the floor.

"You can say that again."

"It's pretty scary."

"Yeah."

I flopped down on the couch. I could feel it sticking to my whole body. My mom kept it covered with plastic, except when company came over. Not my company, of course. Hers. But that was all right. We were allowed to eat in the living room because it was covered. As long as we cleaned up after ourselves.

We bought that couch when my dad was working at the gas station. Before it closed down. Seems like the couch lasted a lot longer than that job. Though, of course, it wasn't his fault the gas station went out of business. Maybe he should have had a job at a liquor store instead. There are more liquor stores than gas stations in West Oakland. That's for sure.

"There's civil wars in countries I never even heard of," Ty said, his eyes glued to the TV again.

"Where they at?"

"Mom and Dad?"

"Yeah."

"In back."

"How come?"

"They stopped fighting, I guess."

"So what are they doing in their room?"

Ty shrugged his shoulders.

"Again?" I whispered. "In the middle of the day?"

"I don't know. I was watching TV."

"Real loud, I bet."

Yeah, I knew what they were doing. So did Ty. The walls of the apartments in the project are not that thick. In case you don't learn about the facts of life from your friends, it's pretty easy to find out what's going on from your parents, if you just keep your mouth shut and your ears open.

"What's to eat?" I asked.

"Thought you had lunch," Ty said.

"Did, but I'm hungry," I said, walking into the kitchen. Ty followed me. I felt a little guilty about being

27

hungry since I'd just eaten an ice cream cone, but my stomach seems to be growing as fast as the rest of me.

I pulled a bag of chips out of the cupboard.

"Pimple food," I said, chomping on a big one.

Just as I picked up another chip, I heard a scream and a crash. Ty and I both jumped. A minute later my dad comes running past the kitchen, zipping up his pants, and he slams out the front door.

Ty and I looked at each other, but we didn't say anything. Ty reached for the bag of chips. We both chewed in rhythm.

Before we could decide what to do next, Mom came running after Dad, pulling on her old, worn-out, silk bathrobe my dad got her for Christmas about five years ago.

I can see she doesn't have any clothes on under the robe, and I'm embarrassed for her. Not for me. I don't care, but for her. She never walks around the house that way. She's always telling me to put some clothes on if I wander around in a T-shirt and underpants. So I know she's upset. Actually, all you have to do is take one look at her face, and you know she's upset.

"I'm going out," Ty says, nervously grabbing the bag of chips from me.

"I hate him," my mom whispers under breath, like she doesn't remember I'm there.

At first I think she's talking about Ty, then I realize she's talking about my dad.

I got very nervous. Not that she didn't have the right to say that, or feel it for that matter, but she'd never said anything like that out loud before. No matter what, she always pretends everything's fine. I mean, we know it isn't. Me and Ty. But we pretend, too. It's easier that way. And besides it *is* fine most of the time. It's just that sometimes when she wants to do something he doesn't want her to do, and she really wants to do it bad, there are some problems. No worse than other people's maybe, but still, problems. Not like the problems Deandra has with her boyfriend. He beats her up about twice a week. My dad just loses his temper once in a while.

Suddenly, my mom collapsed onto one of the kitchen stools and started to cry. I just stood there, really freaked out. I didn't know what to do. Or what to say. I was scared as hell.

"He thinks he has the right to control everything," she said when she pulled herself together. "But I'm sick and tired of giving in to him."

I tried to make myself invisible. Somehow I knew she'd be sorry she'd said that when she felt better. No matter what, she never said anything bad about my dad. Hell, I'm not sure she even thought it. She was that kind of person. They might fight, and all, but I don't think she ever thought he was a bad guy, even though Ty and I sometimes did.

"Sometimes I think I ought to walk out that door and never come back," she said softly.

I shivered. I knew she didn't really mean it, but it scared me, anyway. I couldn't imagine what my life would be like without my mother. Sure, I got mad at her sometimes, and sometimes I wished she'd get off my case, but if she just disappeared on me like Natonia's mother, I'd die. Plain and simple. I'd just die.

"I don't think you ought to tell me about your fights with my dad," I said sharply.

"You're a big girl now, Kisha. You can hear the truth," she said almost angrily.

I knew she was angry at me 'cause I said that to her, and I was angry at myself, too, because it wasn't what I meant to say. But deep down, I really didn't want her to confide in me. It was too much of a responsibility, and I wasn't ready for it. I might have grown out of my clothes, but I was still a kid.

I pretended I was thirsty. I walked over to the sink and poured myself a glass of water, but I could barely drink it down. I kept my back to her, hoping she'd get up and go back to her room. Go anywhere as long as I didn't have to see the look on her face.

At the same time I just wanted to crawl inside that silk

bathrobe, lay my head on my mother's breast, and stay that way forever.

Maybe he'll never come back, I thought. *Maybe this time he's walked out the door for good. Maybe we'll all be better off.*

I knew, of course, that would never happen. *He'll be back tonight,* I thought. *He'll probably be drunk. He'll smile at her and purr in her ear until he makes her laugh. Then she'll forget all the things she said about him and all the things she felt.*

So what was I supposed to do? What was I supposed to say? I hated him for making her so sad. But I also loved him because he could be fun and funny and would always buy us things we couldn't afford just 'cause he wanted to. Like the silk robe he bought my mom, or the pink ballet slippers he bought me. Even though I never took a ballet lesson in my life and have two left feet.

But he wasn't like her. Not deep down. Deep down she was soft, just like she was on the surface, but he was hard. Not mean, exactly. Hard. You could see it in his eyes sometimes, and in the way his thick nostrils flared when he was angry. Like the anger was coming from way down deep inside.

"I'm getting out of here," my mother said, as she lifted herself off the stool.

"No," I said, flinging myself at her. "Don't leave me."

She pulled me off of her roughly. "What ever made you think I was leaving you?" she asked, as if she herself hadn't just said less than five minutes ago that she felt like walking out the door. "I'm going to get dressed so I can cook dinner."

I should have felt relieved, I guess, but I didn't. I felt hatred. I hated her for humiliating me like that. And I vowed if she ever tried to say anything against my father again, I would refuse to listen.

5

Like I thought he would, he came home late last night, way after me and Ty had gone to bed — but not to sleep. Ty was asleep. Or else he was pretending, just like me. I heard my dad knocking around out there, bouncing off the walls. Literally. Until he found his way to the bedroom. Then I heard whispers and muffled sounds for a long time. Not like they were arguing, exactly. The sounds were slow and drawn out, like humming.

Finally I fell asleep, but I woke up two or three times during the night. The humming was still going on. How could they have so much to talk about?

I was exhausted when I got out of bed in the morning, but I was sick of just lying there, so I wandered into the kitchen and sat down at the counter to wait for breakfast. Ty was still asleep. I waited forever, but my mom didn't come in to do her usual thing. It was the same routine every morning: She'd come in, shake her head to get out the cobwebs, and warn us not to talk to her until she'd had her cup of coffee. Some mornings she had two before she said anything, but she'd keep busy the whole time. Making coffee, putting toast in the oven, getting the jelly out, making hot oatmeal. Hot oatmeal! Even in the middle of summer. She'd read somewhere it kept you from getting some kind of disease, or something. We hated it.

But here it was eight-thirty, and there wasn't a sound in the apartment. And I was getting hungry.

Nine o'clock, Ty comes wandering in. "Where's Mom?"

I shrug my shoulders, but I'm getting annoyed just sitting there staring out the window.

Finally, she came in, yawning, and wrapping her robe around her. She walks over to the coffee pot and gets it going. But she was doing everything in slow motion, and it was driving me crazy.

"I've been up since eight-thirty," I said, ignoring the fact that the coffee hadn't even brewed yet. You get used to certain routines, whether you like them or not.

She looked over at me, but she didn't say a word. I slipped off the stool and went over to the phone to call Natonia.

This, of course, was one of Natonia's moody days. "Yes." "No." "Not today." "See you."

I went back to the stool and sat down. Mom pushed a bowl of oatmeal in front of me. Then she slid a piece of toast in my direction, but it was burned. She was, to say the least, off her rhythm today. Usually, everything just slid along the counter from her to me, and it was perfect.

"This isn't a restaurant, Kisha," she said after she'd finished her second cup of coffee. "No reason you can't make your own breakfast."

"But I thought you liked to make it," I grumbled.

"I do," she said. "But you're old enough to make your own breakfast from now on."

"Oh yeah? Who says?"

"I do," she said, taking her coffee and walking out of the room.

A second later she peeked her head back in. I was sure she was going to apologize. "And furthermore, you can watch your mouth, young lady," she said. "I don't like that kind of smart talk."

My mouth dropped open. Damn.

"Did you hear that?" I asked Ty.

"We could do it together. It's not such a big deal," he said.

"That's not the point!" I yelled. "She always makes breakfast. That's the way it is."

"Not anymore," he said.

I ate my toast in silence, gulped down my milk, and threw the oatmeal in the sink, washing most of it down the drain.

Nine o'clock. I had a whole day ahead of me with nothing to do.

I went outside and sat down on the stoop in front of the apartment. I could read a book, which is what my mother always tells me to do when I'm bored. But I didn't feel like it. I could watch TV, but I didn't feel like doing that either. I couldn't stand another rerun.

I decided to just wander around.

Before I knew it, I was right in front of the community center. Darren was standing on the so-called basketball court, which was no more than a pole with a hoop on the top, stuck into cement. He picked up a basketball and shoved it into the basket. First try.

"Been waiting for you," he said.

"Me?"

"Yeah. You. I was hoping you'd show up."

"Looks like nobody else did," I said.

"Then Mohammed will go to the mountain," he said, walking over to me.

"Huh?"

"If they don't come to me, I'll go to them," he explained.

"You know where everyone lives?"

"No, but you're going to tell me."

"I didn't really show up either," I said. "I just happened to be passing by."

"On your way to Natonia's?"

"Not exactly."

"Well, as long as no one showed up, we might as well take a walk. Since this is only my third day here, I don't know where anything is, and I'd appreciate it if you'd show me around the place."

"I'll show you around for a while," I said. "Then I got other things to do." I didn't want to appear to be too anxious. And I sure didn't want him to think I was going to be on any track team, running my head off in this heat.

We automatically started walking in the direction of Natonia's place. Mainly because it was almost directly across the street, and because we both saw her come outside and sit down on the stoop, though it didn't seem like she saw us. It seemed she was more or less looking right through us like we were ghosts or something. Which was pretty freaky.

When we got right up in front of her, she kind of jumped. Like she really hadn't seen us coming.

"How you doing?" Darren asked quietly.

I was impressed. He knew just how to say it. If he'd

been really enthusiastic, if he'd said, "HOW YOU DOING?" and slapped her on the leg, she'd have given him some sarcastic answer. But he kept his distance, and he said it nice and slow. Soft. Smooth. Wrapping it around her like a piece of velvet.

Natonia looked at him for a long minute, as if she wasn't used to people talking to her that way.

"Okay, I guess," she answered, without really looking at either of us.

"I was wondering if you could do me a favor," he said in that same quiet tone of voice.

"Everybody wants a favor from me," Natonia said.

She said it real quietly, but she had a sad look on her face, not a belligerent one like you'd expect. And she still hadn't looked at either of us.

Darren sat down on the stoop next to her. She moved over. Not so much to give him room, as to avoid any physical contact.

"I got hired for this job," he told her, "but if I can't get anyone to participate in any of the activities, I'll get fired."

"You could get another job," Natonia said. "Why would you want to hang out around here, anyway? You obviously don't belong here."

"Do you?"

"I don't belong any place," Natonia said.

"If we had a track team, you'd belong to that," Darren explained.

Natonia didn't say anything. I held my breath, like something really important was going down, though I couldn't exactly tell you what it was.

"Can't have a team with two people and a coach," Natonia said with a snort.

"Kisha's going to show me around the project. Maybe we'll run into a few more girls."

Natonia shrugged her shoulders. "Kisha's going to show you around the project? You might as well go by yourself. She isn't allowed to walk on Filbert. She isn't allowed over to the other side of the center walkway."

I swear I could have killed Natonia at that moment. I was so mad at her for making me out to be a baby. Telling him I wasn't allowed to do this or that. I felt like telling her how my mother confided in me last night, and how she told me I was old enough to make my own breakfast this morning. I didn't need her permission to walk anywhere I wanted to walk anymore. I wasn't a child.

"Then I really need your help," Darren said before I had a chance to protest. "I need both your help."

"You got Natonia now," I pointed out. "You don't need me anymore."

"Are you kidding?" Darren said. "You were the first

person who showed up. We're going to build the team around you.''

I grinned in spite of myself, even though I had no idea what that meant exactly or even if he was telling the truth. I also grinned because he had obviously forgotten about my two left feet.

"And since Natonia already has all those medals, she probably knows about as much as I do, and she can help me demonstrate to the other girls how to do fast walking and jumping jacks and all the exercises you'll be doing.''

"You mean, be your assistant?'' Natonia asked, looking at him for the first time.

"Exactly,'' Darren said.

Well, Natonia could do that all right even if she didn't know a damn thing about track. She knew all there was to know about telling people what to do and how to do it.

"I guess I could show you around a little,'' Natonia said, getting up from the stoop.

I wasn't sure whether to be mad at her for taking my job or happy that she decided to come along with me and Darren.

We headed down one of the walkways toward the opposite side of the project, exactly the place I liked to avoid.

Everyone knew that for some reason this was the part of the project where the drug scene was the worst.

It was like an island of unreality in the middle of the projects, where everyone was high on one thing or another. There were all kinds of rumors about what went on, but like Natonia said, I didn't spend much time around here. It was even worse than where the Johnsons lived.

"You know Alisha," Natonia said, pointing to one of the buildings near by. "She lives over there."

She walked up the stairs of the stoop.

"You going right in?" I asked, looking around.

Natonia gave me one of her looks and knocked on the door. Darren and I stood on the bottom step.

A weird-looking woman with a black sweater wrapped around her, despite the heat, opened the door. She shielded her eyes from the sun and barked at Natonia.

"Whatchu want, girl?"

"Alisha home?" Natonia asked, without batting an eyelash.

Alisha came to the door, and squeezed past her mother.

"You ain't going nowhere. I need you to help me out," her mother said.

"No one can help you out," Alisha said sharply. "Except the candy man, and he won't be around till three, so you'll just have to hang in there till then.''

"We got money to pay him?''

"You got your welfare check yesterday,'' Alisha said, taking it out of her pocket. "I'll go cash it for you.''

Alisha's mother grunted, then she walked back into the almost empty apartment without even closing the door.

Natonia was introducing Alisha to Darren, but I was still watching Alisha's mother. She picked up a bottle from the top of the TV, put it up to her mouth, and drank it down. Then she shook her head and shivered.

Alisha, glad for an excuse to get out of the house, shifted from one foot to the other while she talked to Darren. *She'd probably be real good for the team,* I thought, *since she can never stand still, let alone sit still.*

So I felt good when Alisha said she'd join the group. She also said we should go get Tureena, who was a great runner. She'd had plenty of practice running away from home.

We ran into Tureena on Filbert Street. I almost fainted. She was standing with the homeboys we'd seen yesterday. The drug dealers. Alisha pulled her to the side and whispered something to her. Tureena looked at Darren, and shook her head. Then she whispered something back.

"Later,'' Alisha said as she walked back toward us.

"My mom's waiting for you," she said to the guy standing next to Tureena as we walked past. I remembered what Natonia had said about pointing, and I kept my hands in my pockets.

Alisha explained that Tureena was with her boyfriend, and he didn't like her talking to other guys. This struck me as pretty funny. Darren wasn't exactly another guy. He was an adult.

Neither Natonia nor Alisha nor I could come up with anyone else, but we could hardly have a team with only three girls. We were walking back toward my house, shaking our heads, when I suddenly remembered the Barton twins.

"I know!" I shouted.

The Barton twins were really, really smart. The smartest kids in our class. They knew just about everything, and they were tall, too. Plus, they were nice. They never gave anyone any lip. I felt a lot more comfortable with them than I did with Alisha or Tureena. But, of course, they weren't nearly as interesting or exciting as Natonia.

They were home playing Scrabble, no less, and they were totally thrilled with the idea of a track team. So were their parents. Their father was this really old man who used to be a high school track coach in his day, and their mom was a kind of pretty, washed-out-looking white woman who never said much.

They joined us and suggested Esther, who didn't actually live in the project, but close by. She was a friend of theirs from school. We all walked over to Esther's. She was baby-sitting her younger sisters and brothers. About ten of them. But the apartment was nice and clean, like ours. She said her mom was at work. Alisha and Natonia made some crude remarks about that, but Esther pushed her glasses back on her nose and explained that her mother was a legal secretary, and she worked in an office.

Everyone introduced Darren and told her why we were there. Esther listened carefully, and gave it some thought.

"I have to see if Miriam will stay with the younger kids," she explained. "She's oldest next to me. And I have to be home by four."

She called out to Miriam.

Miriam agreed to baby-sit in exchange for wearing Esther's new blouse the first day of school.

We walked outside, and I realized we suddenly had six girls. I didn't know how many we needed for a team, but it looked like we might be on our way.

Darren leaned over to me as we walked back to the center. "Thanks," he said. "You got the ball rolling."

Well, that's what happens when you take responsibility, I thought, but I didn't say anything.

6

"Let's jog back to the center," Darren suggested.

My heart dropped. Now he'd see what a turkey I was, and I'd be off the team before I even got on it.

Everyone started to run. They all looked like gazelles, of course. I held up the rear. Puff, puff, puff. Out of breath before we rounded the corner. Tripping over my own feet, as usual.

We made it back to the center, and Darren looked so pleased with himself I could have thrown up.

"You're not even breathing hard," he said to us. "Let's continue on."

Maybe you're *not breathing hard,* I thought, *but I am.* No one complained though, so on we went, in a straight line like six little ducklings waddling after the father duck. Five of them happy to be there. Me — suddenly wishing I was home listening to music.

And where did we go? Right back up Filbert Street. Before yesterday I never even walked on Filbert if I could help it. And today I'm jogging down it, like it's a perfectly natural thing to do.

We pass by Tureena's boyfriend, and he stares at us. It gives me the creeps. I try not to look at him. Natonia gives him the "V" sign, and he salutes her back. I feel a little better, but it strikes me as kind of strange that they use the peace sign. On second thought, maybe it's not so strange. Anytime those freaks want to start a drug war, or any other kind of war, I guess they can.

We pass by a boarded-up apartment building facing the street.

Darren turns around and starts jogging backwards. "Looks like there was a fire there," he says, pointing to the apartment.

Alisha and Natonia start to giggle.

I start to warn him not to point. Then I get too embarrassed to say anything. It sounds so stupid.

"Somebody fell asleep cooking!" Alisha yells.

"Blew the windows out," Natonia says, and she starts to laugh.

Darren looks confused. Everyone laughs. Even I know what they're talking about, and I'm certainly not "street." He turns, faces forward again, and picks up speed.

"Cooking crack," Alisha says. "One of the hazards of the trade."

Darren shakes his head and sprints ahead of us. He's wearing shorts and a T-shirt, and I can see that his legs are thick and powerful. His shoulders and arms are muscular, like an athlete's. He looks good. The only problem is he's so naive you'd think he was a white man.

By the time we jogged back to the center again, I was totally done in. I lay down on the cement and started to moan, but Darren said we had to cool down, not just stop suddenly, so I pulled myself up — Lord knows how I managed to do that — and we slowly circled around in front of the center for a few minutes, then headed into the building for a meeting.

Tureena was standing inside the doorway, looking a little nervous, but Darren just gave her the high sign and told her he was glad she could join us. I wasn't sure I agreed with him, given the company she kept, but if he could get me to run, he could perform miracles, so I wasn't about to question anything he said at this point.

"If we're having a meeting, I want to be the president," Natonia said.

Darren said it wasn't that kind of meeting, that in this group everyone was equal and had an equal say. This, of course, was very appealing to all of us, except Natonia, who wanted to be more equal than anybody else.

We sat down in a circle on the floor. There wasn't any

furniture in the place to speak of, just a couple of old folding chairs.

Darren told us he was going to set up a schedule and post it on the bulletin board. I must say I was surprised to see that there was a bulletin board in the center and that the place had actually been cleaned out. It wasn't exactly a palace, but it was an improvement. With a bucket of paint and some window washing — where there were windows and not boards — it wouldn't be half bad. Someone had even cut out some pictures from magazines and pasted them up on the walls. Mostly religious stuff.

"We're going to start our daily exercise routine to-morrow morning at nine sharp," Darren said. "We'll start with simple exercises and work our way up, then we'll run a mile, come back, and do some more exercises."

Everyone groaned.

"It sounds a lot harder than it is," he said. "By the third week, we'll be running three miles a day. By the fourth week, four. And by the sixth week — "

"No. Don't say it," Alisha whined. "We'll never be able to do that."

"Yes, we will," the Barton twins said at the same time.

We all tried to shout them down. Six miles a day, and

we'd be dead. "If *you're* so hot to run, *you* run six miles a day, Twins. We'll watch!" Natonia cried.

Everybody just called them Twins, cause nobody could tell them apart. I guess I knew their other names once, but I couldn't remember them anymore, and neither could anybody else. Even when you ran into only one of them, which was rare, you'd just say, "Hi, Twin." They didn't mind.

"And what about lunch?" Alisha asked. "We can't exercise all day and not eat.

"Bring it with you," Darren said. "You'll be here all day. Every weekday. And Saturday mornings. Sundays off."

"We're running on Saturdays?" Tureena groaned.

"What are you groaning about?" Natonia said. "You haven't even done anything yet. We're the ones who ran our asses off today."

"It's just that Saturday morning's after Friday night," Tureena said.

"Now that is really big news," Natonia said.

"I like to stay in bed till noon on Saturday," Tureena whined.

We all laughed.

"I don't know about the rest of you all, but I get it on on Friday nights," Tureena said angrily. "So I say we vote."

"If we're going to have a team, we're going to have to practice six days a week," Darren said firmly.

Well, that was the first rule, I guess. It looked as if at least Darren was going to be more than equal. I held my breath waiting for someone to challenge him. Nobody did.

Before the meeting was dismissed, we tried a few stretching exercises. Darren called them yogi, or something like that. He let Natonia demonstrate how to do something called the cat, and she loved that, of course.

When I looked at my watch, it was almost three o'clock. No wonder I was hungry.

"See you all tomorrow," Darren said, after we'd lain on our backs with our eyes closed and relaxed for a few minutes.

Nobody moved.

He laughed softly.

Slowly, we all pulled ourselves together and walked outside.

"That was fun," the Barton twins said.

"Passed the time," Tureena said.

"Damn, I gotta get to the store and cash that check," Alisha called, as she ran out the door.

"I'll walk you," I said to Natonia, whose mood had obviously passed. "I hope you got something to eat at your house. I'm starving."

"I got some chores to do," Natonia said a little anxiously. "I'll see you tomorrow."

I knew she wasn't telling me the truth, but I didn't know why. I hated it when she did that to me. Especially after we'd had such a nice day.

I walked home slowly even though I was so hungry I wished I'd eaten the damn oatmeal for breakfast. And I was a little upset, too. I couldn't put my finger on it, but something was wrong with Natonia. She was moody. Always had been. But this was something different. She was moody *and* angry. It was like she couldn't stand to be around me all the time anymore. Before, we couldn't stand to be apart from each other. We'd even sleep in the same twin bed on weekends. We weren't allowed to during the week because of school. But all spring we talked about her sleeping over during the week, too, as soon as school was out.

Natonia always slept at my house because she didn't actually have a place to sleep at her grandmother's. Her grandmother slept in this real tiny room, and her two uncles slept in the big bedroom. Natonia slept on the couch most of the time. Sometimes she slept in her grandmother's bed, but her grandmother snored, so she preferred the couch.

Lately, however, you'd think she was tied to that couch, or something. She never wanted to sleep over.

When I'd ask her to, she'd get all mad. Once I said I'd sleep over at her place. That I'd bring my blanket and sleep on the floor next to the couch, but she about freaked out, so I never brought that up again.

We used to tell each other everything. We did everything together. Everything! We both got our periods for the first time in the very same week. My mom took us out for lunch to celebrate. And she really splurged and bought us each a pair of fancy underpants. We pretended she was crazy, that getting your period wasn't anything to celebrate, but afterward we told each other it was really nice. It made us feel good. Special. Which is exactly what my mother intended, I guess. Only we didn't realize it at the time. We were too embarrassed.

Now, every time I get my period, I wonder if Natonia's getting hers, but I never ask anymore.

The house was real quiet when I came in. I wondered what Ty had done all day. He usually didn't run out so early in the morning unless he absolutely had to. Even when my mom asked him to go next door and borrow some milk, he tried to think of every excuse not to. It wasn't that he was lazy, or anything, but, as I said before, he just has this thing about going outside. Unless he's with my mom or dad. Then he feels protected.

"That you, Kisha?" my mom called out from her bedroom.

"Yeah. I'm starved!" I yelled.

"There's half a tuna sandwich in the fridge."

I inhaled the tuna sandwich in two seconds, then I walked back to my mother's bedroom. She was sitting on the bed, going through a box of stuff.

"Where's Ty?"

"He and your dad went to the store."

I looked around the room. Everything seemed to be in place. She was dressed. The bed was made. She didn't look any different from the way she usually looked. It was like everything that went on last night and this morning was a dream.

I waited for her to ask me what I did all day.

"I've been going through some of my stuff from high school," my mother said. "I found this paper I wrote for my English class senior year. It's good. I forgot how much I used to like to write."

Well, that was it. She'd flipped out. Who in her right mind would keep a paper she wrote for an English class fifteen years ago?

"I got an A on the paper, and it says here that it's excellent."

"What's it about?" I asked suspiciously. There was obviously some reason she was showing me this paper. It probably had to do with good manners, or something.

53

"It's a book report."

"Maybe I can copy it if we have to read the same book," I said, and I laughed. That was something she'd really let me do. Never.

She hit me over the head with the paper. "You don't have to copy my stuff. You're smart enough on your own," she said.

I guess I was forgiven.

"How come you're looking through that old stuff now, anyway?"

"I'm looking for my high school diploma."

My mouth dropped open. There's only one reason for anyone to look for her high school diploma, and it isn't so she can frame it and put it up on the wall.

7

I got up, but Ty was still sleeping. There wasn't a sound in the house. I did what I had to do, then I walked into the kitchen and waited around for a few minutes. Still no sign of life, so I made my breakfast, oatmeal and all, laced up my tennis shoes, and headed for the community center. I felt good this morning. I felt great. I'd run yesterday. I'd done exercises, and nobody had told me I was a turkey. Maybe I was growing out of it.

My mom suddenly appeared in the kitchen as I was on my way out the door. I felt really mad at her. I thought she was just waiting for me to leave before she came in to get her coffee. That way she wouldn't have to make breakfast or talk to me. I started to shoot her a dirty look from the doorway, but she just smiled at me and told me to have a good day. Even before she had her coffee. The mean kind of melted out of me. I guess I liked the way she said, "Have a good day." Made me feel really proud. I had a place to go. It was almost like having a job.

Naturally, I was the first to arrive at the community center. The door was locked. Bolted, actually. Obviously Darren hadn't gotten there yet, so I hung around outside waiting for him.

I picked up a few stones and tried them out on the cement. Finally, I found one good enough for writing, and I just kind of let my hand do whatever it wanted to, without thinking.

I drew a heart and inside I wrote "Kisha loves Darren." When I looked at it, it gave me a start. And it was also crazy. Darren was a grown-up man.

I tried to rub it out with my shoe, but it wouldn't come off. Panic. Natonia was Miss Eagle-Eye herself. She'd see it, no doubt, and announce it to the entire world, and I'd never hear the end of it. And, of course, I'd have to drop off the track team because I'd be totally mortified.

I spit on the heart until I couldn't get one more drop of saliva out of my mouth, then I tried rubbing it out again. I managed to get rid of my name just as this big, new car with four doors pulled up nearby. There's not exactly a parking place in front of the center, but there's room to park — sort of — on the so-called basketball court.

I forget about the rest of the heart. I wonder if some kind of drug pusher is driving that car, and I'm getting nervous. I know for a fact the only people who drive big, new cars around here are pushers and the minister of our church. I get my fingers ready to make a peace sign, just in case, and I start looking around for Darren, hoping he'll show up. But I don't even know what direction he'll be coming from.

Suddenly, the door opens, and Darren pops out of the car.

I give him the eye. Darren? I know he's not a minister. At least I don't think he is. Could he be — ? Nah.

He's waving at me, like he has no idea I'm thinking bad thoughts. Then he walks over to where I'm standing.

"You guys gotta get some decent track shoes," he says, looking at my beat-up tennis shoes.

"What's track shoes?"

"With cleats on the bottom."

"Can you wear 'em to school?"

"Not exactly," he says, laughing. "They're just for running outdoors."

"Then we won't be buying any of those," I said. "I

get new tennis shoes at the beginning of every school year. Track shoes aren't exactly in the budget."

Darren looks at me, kind of embarrassed. I look at the car. Obviously, this is a guy who never had to worry about a budget. Probably lives up in the hills, or in Berkeley, even. And again I wonder what he's doing at Whitman. *He's squeaky clean. Even his gym shorts are pressed. He's never gonna last here,* I think sadly.

By nine-thirty, everyone's milling around, ready to go. We start with warm-up exercises. Stretches mostly. Nice and slow. I'm doing them, just like everyone else. Well, maybe not exactly like everyone else, but I'm doing them.

"Okay," Darren says. "We're going to run around the perimeter of the project. We'll start slowly, so you won't get winded and peak too early. And we'll keep a nice steady pace."

I swallow hard and take my place at the end of the jogging line. *If I have to stop and walk, I will,* I tell myself. *Who you kidding?* I ask. *You know you'd rather die than do that.*

I start off with high hopes, anyway. But about two blocks into the run, I realize it wasn't going to be any easier today than yesterday. I'm already dragging behind. Everyone else is about half a block ahead of me. I feel like turning around and going home. Then I see

Darren's slowing down a little. Everyone else slows down, too, but I keep a steady pace. I'm almost up to them.

And I fall in love with him, for sure, right then and there, because I know Darren has slowed down just for me. But he's acting like it's just part of the routine.

I am totally high on our little secret.

But as I approach the others, I notice they're right in front of the crack house, jogging in place.

I coax myself into picking up some speed, and I catch up to them at the same time some dude with dreadlocks comes running out of the crack house — toting a gun.

I stop short, I'm shaking all over.

Everyone else stops moving, too. We're just staring at the dude because he's heading straight for Darren.

"Whatchu think you're doing here?" he yells at Darren.

"We're jogging," Darren says calmly, like he doesn't even notice the gun.

"Well, jog someplace else, Oreo," the guy says to Darren. "You ain't got no business here. People see you and your little ladies, they'll stay away. Find someplace else to do your jogging."

For emphasis, the guy points the gun straight at Darren. I about fainted, but Darren suddenly looks like he's ready to explode. Now I'm really scared. Doesn't he know people get whacked around here if they get in the way. Hell, the security guard wound up with fifteen bullet holes in him. Everybody talked about it for months. Now there's no guard. No one else would take the job.

I want to run, but I can't. I want to hold up my two fingers and make a peace sign, but I can't get my arms to move from my sides. *Why doesn't Natonia do something?* I wonder. I want to yell to Darren. I want to warn him. But I can't say a word. Time just kind of stands still, like in a movie when the action suddenly stops for a minute, and the characters are frozen on the screen. That's what it feels like. Like we're all in a movie. Because this can't really be happening to us. It's weird. Like my mind detached itself from my body, and I'm there, but not there.

Part of me felt like we'd been standing in front of the crack house forever, but I don't think more than a few seconds passed. At some level, however, my mind registered that Darren is furious. For a moment it's just a feeling, then the feeling is verified.

In a flash, Darren raises his arm and knocks the gun out of the other guy's hand. He wrestles him to the ground, then he smashes him in the stomach a few times. Hard.

We're all stunned. Mainly cause it happened so fast.

60

But mostly because it happened at all. Even if this isn't the safest place in the world to live, you never think anything like this is really going to happen to you. Or to anyone you really know. I mean, I knew the security guard, but I didn't really *know* him. Just said "hi" a few times.

"Stay out of our faces, and we'll stay out of yours," Darren says. Then he gets up, and, without saying another word, starts slowly jogging down the street.

"Come on!" Natonia yells.

We fall into line and follow. Darren runs real slow until he hits the corner, and then he picks up speed and we head back to the community center. I'm shaking all over, and not because I'm tired from running. I forgot all about that. And for sure I don't intend to lag behind. I'm right up there, running next to Esther. I don't want to be last in line even if I drop dead of a heart attack.

When we get to the center, Esther's sister Miriam is standing there with her hands on her hips, and Esther breaks out of line and runs over to her.

"Uoooo," Miriam says. "You're gonna get it. Mama was looking all over for you. You know it's Saturday and you're not allowed — "

"Just shut up," Esther whispers fiercely.

"I gotta go," she yells to Darren, and she pushes Miriam out of the way and starts running.

Mind you, Esther is not the kind of kid who would ordinarily do a thing like that, so we're all kind of shook up all over again. Mainly because we're still shook up from what went on with Darren on Filbert. But nobody says anything. We just go into the center and grab our lunches. Everyone's really quiet. Most of us just pretend to eat.

Monday, I walked to the center. I had seen the twins and Natonia on Sunday but none of us said anything about what happened on Saturday. And it wasn't because we forgot. I don't think I'll ever be able to forget that dude pointing his gun at Darren.

But when everyone showed up on Monday, that was the first thing we talked about. Like maybe we finally had to make sure that what we saw was real. And it actually did feel more real when we went over all the events together.

None of us, of course, had told our parents. My mom, for one, would never have let me come back. Being on the track team would have been history with a capital H. Same for the twins. We were sure Darren would find another route for us to run.

We told him he was a hero, and we could see he kind of liked that, but he was real modest, too. He told us he was no hero. He said it's not right to beat up people, and he doesn't believe in violence. But he also said sometimes you have to defend your rights and let certain people know they can't run the world. Then he kind of stared into space, like he was thinking about something else.

We all agreed and told him he was a hero whether he wanted to be or not.

After we talked it out, we all felt better. It was a relief to talk about things. Sometimes you just have to, or you'll explode.

We did our warm-ups and headed outside. And wouldn't you know it, he starts out on the very same route. We head right for Filbert Street. My heart almost jumped out of my chest.

I see the crack house coming up, and I close my eyes. No doubt about it, I'm scared, Darren or no Darren. Hero or no hero.

I open my eyes just in time to see another guy, a really mean-looking dude, come out of the house as we approach. And I think *This is it. This time the guy's prepared, and Darren's gonna get whacked for sure.*

Instead, this homeboy's walking toward us, swinging his hands at his sides. No gun. He has one tooth missing in front, but he has this big smile on his face. And he yells at a group of junkies standing on the sidewalk, "Track team coming through. Everybody out of the way."

8

The rest of the summer just sort of slipped by. I knew one thing for sure, though. It was the best summer of my life. I felt — full. That was the only way to describe it: Like my life had some definite purpose.

I worked out with the team every day except Sunday. So almost every day I had someplace to go. We were a real group, and Darren thought we'd be ready to compete with other teams in the fall.

But the thing was, we still couldn't really figure Darren out. Was he "street," or wasn't he? He didn't look street. Didn't act street. But he wasn't afraid of anything, or anybody. Not that he shoved people around, or yelled at them, or flexed his muscles — unless he had to. He just had this — presence. This really strong presence. He never said much, but when he talked, after a while, we all sort of listened. I don't know why. Maybe because he believed in us.

Of course, along about the middle of August, when I decided I might take a chance and tell Natonia that I was totally in love with Darren, he showed up at practice one Saturday afternoon with this woman named Lureen — which was bad enough — but in her arms was a baby. Darren's baby! I about died.

I knew it was stupid, but I wanted to lie right down and cry, I was so hurt.

Then I quickly counted back and realized that Lila was over a year old. They had the baby before Darren even met me. So I felt better about it. But that didn't keep me from hating the woman's guts.

It came out later that they actually lived together, which, of course, was the right thing for him to do, but since Darren was so proper, and all, I was surprised they weren't married.

Basically, I learned a lot of things that summer. I learned to *do* things. All kinds of things I never thought I'd be able to do. I still wasn't the fastest runner in the group, that's for sure, but I could jump, and I could do stairs without huffing and puffing, and I was a lot more flexible than I thought I was. Plus, I was really toned. My muscles had muscles. There wasn't an ounce of baby fat left on my body. If only I could have done something with my hair, my life would have been complete.

Natonia continued to be a little weird, but I figured she was going through some growing-up process, too, and I'd just have to put up with it until she got her act together. Not that it didn't hurt my feelings. It did. She was still my best friend. But I had other friends now, too. I even liked Alisha and Tureena. And everyone loved the twins. Esther was the quietest one in the group. She was always polite to everyone, but she seemed kind of different. Maybe because she didn't live in the project, like the rest of us.

One day we were running at the Oakland track, which always made me feel special — I mean who'd have thought old turkey feet could run four miles around a track? And there was this white girl running so fast you could barely see her feet touching the ground. She had the longest legs I'd ever seen on a human being. Longer than Natonia's even. She whizzed past like she'd been zapped with an electrical current, and, damn, she wasn't even breathing hard.

After we finished running, we stood around and watched her for a while. Then this older man with blond, curly hair came up to Darren and introduced himself.

"I'm Patrick Dunne," he says, holding out his hand.

"I've been watching your girls run. They're good. Better than any of the kids on Jennifer's team at school."

"Thanks," Darren said, and I could see he was really proud of us.

"That's my daughter," this Dunne guy said, pointing to the white girl, still running around the track.

"Looks like she's training for the Olympics," Darren said, half joking.

"You bet," Dunne said.

Only *he* wasn't joking the least bit.

We looked at each other and rolled our eyes. This guy had some big ideas.

"I'm training my girls for the Olympics, too," Darren said.

We about dropped dead on the spot.

"That's what I figured," Dunne said.

We started to giggle. *I could just see me running in the Olympics. Or anyone else standing here,* I thought. *That'd be the day.*

In the meantime, Darren was talking away like he really believed it was a possibility. And this Dunne character was telling him he wanted Jennifer to run with our team.

Darren said, "Sure, we'd love for her to join," and Patrick Dunne said he'd be glad to be Darren's assistant, help him out when he could.

Darren gave him all the information about where to come and stuff. Then the guy called his daughter over when she stopped running the track, and just like that, before you knew it, it was a done deal.

We talked about it all the way back to the center. We weren't sure how we felt about this girl being on the team. For lots of reasons.

One thing — the girl might run like she had a motor built into her system, but she didn't talk. I've seen shy before. I'm shy sometimes myself, but this girl Jennifer was so shy she never even raised her head the whole time her father and Darren were talking. She was so shy she could barely look at Darren when he started talking to her. Either she was the shyest human being on earth, or something worse than that — something none of us cared to mention.

But Darren said we could learn something from her, so we agreed to give it a try even though we weren't all that happy about it.

When we got back to the center, Darren said he wanted to talk to us. "We need track shoes badly," he announced. "We can't compete without them."

We exchanged looks. How were we going to tell him there was no way any of us was going to be able to buy them — except this new girl, Jennifer, maybe. She probably already had them.

My heart dropped. We'd come all this way, but now what? I wanted to laugh and cry at the same time.

"And we're going to find some way to get the money to buy those shoes," Darren said. "I've been thinking about a bake sale, maybe. Any of you guys cook?"

"Me," Alisha said, jumping up. "I can cook."

"Me too," Natonia said.

Everyone was getting in on the act, and in two minutes it was settled. We were going to have a bake sale. Darren was a genius.

We made plans to have it on Saturday afternoon, after training, when the community center was jumping.

Now that the center had been fixed up, and someone had donated a pool table, there were times when a hundred kids showed up. And Darren even had an assistant to help out because lots of times Darren wasn't there. He was busy with us or with the choir he'd started, which Ty belonged to. Or the basketball team for older boys that practiced in the evenings.

There were two rules at the center. No drugs or liquor, and no fighting.

At first some of the kids didn't pay attention to the rules, but they found out they weren't welcome. Darren escorted them to the door and told them to come back when they were clean. A few came back. Others didn't. But no one came back stoned.

All the windows had been replaced, and no one had broken any of the new ones. Someone donated a beat-up old couch, someone else donated paint, and we had spent a weekend painting the place. It was hard to remember how disgusting it used to be.

Darren found out that LaRue, one of the older boys, who was mean as hell, was an excellent artist. He brought LaRue some bright colors and told him to get to work on the outside of the building. Paint a mural. Hell, I didn't even know what a mural was. Neither did LaRue, but Darren explained all about it, and he told the dude he could paint whatever he wanted to.

"What about the track team?" LaRue asked.

Darren said that would be great.

We all pretended we didn't want our faces plastered all over the walls, but it was a trip. LaRue was still working on it, but he'd already done Esther and me, and it looked just like us.

It was like Darren had spread this magic potion over everyone, because people just wanted to act nice and be cool around him.

Even Natonia chilled out. One day she said she wouldn't mind walking me back to my house.

"Sure," I said. I had to bite my tongue to keep myself from asking her if she wanted to sleep over. I was so thrilled that she wanted to be with me. But I didn't want to crowd her.

We walked along for a while. Neither of us said anything. It was like we didn't quite fit together anymore — it was like we were part of a puzzle, but our shapes had changed, and we couldn't quite fit our new shapes into the empty spaces.

"You're still my best friend," Natonia said finally, as if she could read my mind, like in the old days.

"You, too," I said. My throat filled up with tears, and I could hardly talk. I was so grateful.

"There's just things sometimes," she continued.

"Yeah," I said. "I know."

Only I didn't, of course. Though I wished I did.

We walked along some more, but neither of us said anything else, and when we got to my house, she turned and said, "See you tomorrow," and she walked away.

I wanted to call after her. I wanted to ask her what the things were. But I didn't.

I guess all she wanted to do was apologize, and her walking me home accomplished that. And that was all I could expect for now. It was enough. Well, it was and it wasn't. It was, but I was a pig, I guess. I wanted more.

9

My mom was vacuuming the living room when I walked in. I tried to get past her while her back was turned and sneak into my bedroom before she saw me. It's not that I was avoiding her exactly. It was more that I was avoiding the housework — which I must admit I avoided as often as possible. Tyrone's job was to dry the dishes and wash the kitchen floor. Mine was to dust. Everything. Constantly. Including the bedroom floors. Like I was a human Dust Buster. Could I help it if dust balls sprang up overnight and gathered under the beds? How could anyone expect me to spend my whole life chasing after them, day after day? Like I have nothing better to do with my time.

I got about halfway to my room when I felt someone tugging at my shirt.

"Just because you're involved in the track team,

doesn't mean you can shirk your duties at home, Lady,"
my mom said.

She calls me "Lady" when she's irritated as hell at me.

"I just dusted yesterday," I said, trying to pull away
from her.

"More like last week, if you ask me," she said, hanging on to my shirt.

"Well, I'm not asking you," I mumbled.

"What?"

"I said I'll do it as soon as I change my clothes."

"That's what I thought you said."

She let go of my shirt and walked back to the living
room. Lucky for me she hadn't heard what I said. She'd
have Lady'd me right to my room for the next twelve
weeks.

As I shuffled down the hallway, I started getting madder and madder. If I was supposed to be such a grownup, how come I couldn't decide for myself when it was
time to dust?

I threw off my clothes and put on a beat-up pair of
shorts and a T-shirt. I'd been working out all day. The
only thing I wanted to do right now was jump into the
shower, stand there for an hour, and cool off. I promised myself that's exactly what I'd do as soon as I finished dusting.

As I was about to trudge to the kitchen to get the

cleaning stuff, I heard the front door slam. BANG. My dad came stomping into the apartment in a fury, like a bat out of hell. He was yelling and cussing, shouting something that sounded like "over my dead body!" but my mom turned on the vacuum, so I couldn't make out what it was he was actually saying.

A second later, the vacuum went off again, and he shouted that she was running around behind his back.

I froze. Not my mom. Everybody else's mom. Anybody else's mom. But not mine. I was sure of that.

The vacuum went on again.

Then off. He was still yelling.

". . . welfare, like everybody else around here! You think you're better than the rest of us?"

"Of course not," I hear my mother say.

Then I hear her trying to shush my dad.

"Kisha's in back," she whispers.

"I don't give a damn who's in back," he says.

The vacuum went on again for one second.

"Why'd you go and do that?" my mother said angrily. "You know we don't have the money to get it fixed."

"Money, money, money. Is that all you ever think about?" he yelled.

I put my hands over my ears.

"Because we don't have any," my mother shouted.

"What do you want me to do? Rob a bank?"

"Get a job!"

I hear a CRACK. Then my mom cries out.

I couldn't believe my ears. As bad as things get sometimes, my dad's never hit my mom.

I crept out of my room, shaking. I didn't know what I was doing exactly, but I headed for the living room.

Before I got there, I heard the front door slam again.

I peeked around the corner. My mom was standing in the middle of the living room holding the cord to the vacuum cleaner. I could see that the plug was missing. She was just standing there. Slowly, she put her other hand up to her cheek. She was facing me, but she wasn't looking at me. It was as if she was looking inside, not outside.

There was a red handprint on her cheek.

She stiffened up for a moment, then she reached down and picked up something from a mess of papers on the floor. A letter, maybe.

She dropped the broken cord and took the letter into the kitchen.

I just stood there for a long time. I didn't know what to do. I felt so ashamed that my dad would behave like that. I was so embarrassed for my mom. And for me. I felt myself go dizzy with shame.

Finally, I heard the front door open and close again. I could hardly catch my breath.

"Mom?" Tyrone calls out.

Thank goodness.

My mother doesn't answer.

I wanted to signal to him. Tell him to walk past the kitchen and come to the hallway. Let him know in some way that Mom can't answer him now, though I don't really know why. *What's she doing?* I wondered. *Is she deciding whether she should call the police?* Alisha's mom called the police on her boyfriend lots of times. But my mom's not Alisha's mom. My mom's strong, and my dad's —

Part of me wanted her to call the police. Part of me didn't. What would they do? Arrest him? That would be terrible. Everyone would know.

Ty glanced into the kitchen and picked up the vibes. He tiptoed down the hallway and looked at me, like he knew something was going on, but he couldn't figure out what.

I put my finger in front of my lips and motioned for him to follow me to the bedroom.

"What's she doing?" I asked as soon as I closed the door.

"Standing at the counter writing something. What's going on?"

"I don't know. Some kind of fight about her doing something he didn't want her to do because he didn't have a job."

"What?"

"I don't know. It was confusing. It happened so fast, and the vacuum cleaner went on and off."

"You're not telling me because you think I'm too young."

"I'm not telling you because that's all I know," I said, still trying to piece it all together.

"What's she writing?"

"Beats me."

"Should we go in there?"

"Into the kitchen?"

"Yeah."

"Why?"

"To see if she needs anything."

"I don't know."

"Me neither."

We looked at each other. Then we both slumped down on our beds, feeling totally inadequate.

We lay there for a long time without speaking. I wasn't thinking about anything. I don't know if Ty was or not. I was just watching this fly crawl up the wall and over to the window. It was trying to get out, but it kept bumping into the window pane, driving itself crazy, trying and trying to get through the glass. I felt sorry for the stupid fly.

It depressed the hell out of me. I wished I could have

called Natonia. I knew that just the sound of her voice would make me feel better, but somehow I didn't think that was the right thing to do.

"He slapped her," I said finally.

I actually hadn't meant to say it, but I couldn't keep it in anymore. It was too terrible.

Ty didn't say anything. He just turned to look at me.

"He slapped her," I repeated as if I were talking in slow motion. "On the face."

Ty winced.

"Then he ran out. Probably to get drunk, or something."

"I hate him," Ty said.

"Me, too," I whispered.

The whole conversation seemed to be in slow motion now. Ty would say something, then after a while I'd say something. Then a long time would pass, and he'd say something again. It seemed to be taking forever to get our thoughts from our heads to our mouths.

"Sometimes I don't hate him, but I do now."

"Me, too."

"Did she hit him back?"

"No."

Ty got this strange look on his face, as if he was about to cry, but he couldn't, or wouldn't let himself. I figured he was probably feeling embarrassed for Mom, too. I don't know. Maybe that's not what he was thinking at all. I wasn't even sure why I was thinking it.

The next minute he was throwing himself on the bed face down and crying his heart out.

I went over and sat down next to him. I felt big and awkward. I didn't know what to do with my hands. I wasn't sure if I should hug him, or if he'd think I was treating him like a baby. I kind of smoothed down his hair.

"I know. I know," I cooed.

But I didn't know. I didn't know anything. The older I got, the dumber I felt.

"It's my fault," he said, after a long time.

"How could it be your fault?" I asked. "You weren't even here."

"That's the point," he said. And he started whimpering again. "I knew if I left the house something terrible would happen someday. Only I thought it would happen on the outside, not the inside."

"Ty, baby," I said, trying to hug him. "It's not your fault. People aren't supposed to stay in the house all the time. It's not normal. It's good you went out. It's good you weren't here. Honest."

"Not true," he said, pounding the bed.

There was no way I could convince him he wasn't responsible. And the more I tried to convince him *he* wasn't, the more responsible *I* felt. Why had I just stood there, like a fool?

I felt worse and worse.

I wanted my mom to put her arms around me and comfort me.

"I'm going into the kitchen," I said, getting up from the bed.

"What are you gonna say?"

"Nothing. I'm just going in."

I walked down the hallway as quietly as I could. She was still standing at the counter writing. I glanced over at her, but she didn't pay any attention to me. I wasn't sure if she was ignoring me, or if she didn't see me.

I walked over to the broom closet and started to open it. I never noticed that it squeaked before.

I opened it all the way and took out the mop and dust cloth.

Still, she didn't make a move. I cleared my throat. In case she wanted to talk to me, I wanted her to know I was there.

She didn't turn around, so I took the mop and the dust cloth and walked into the living room.

I dusted the TV from top to bottom, every surface — whether you could see it or not. And I dusted every other piece of furniture in that room, as well. Then I dragged the mop along the floor in the hallway and into our bedroom.

Ty was still sprawled out on the bed, but he had stopped crying.

I reached under the beds and dusted until every dust ball had disappeared into the mop. "Must have been a month since I did this," I mumbled to myself.

I felt better. I took the cleaning stuff back to the kitchen. My mom was sealing up an envelope.

"Would you do me a favor?" she asked.

"Anything," I said. And I meant it. I was so glad she was talking to me normal again.

"Go down to the corner and mail this," she said.

"Now?"

"Now," she said. She handed me the letter.

I walked to the door.

"Wait," she called.

I turned around.

"Never mind," she said. "Do it now."

10

I got up early because I wanted to get out of the house as soon as I could. I didn't know if my dad had come back last night or not, and I didn't want to find out, even though by this morning, what happened yesterday felt more like some kind of nightmare than anything real.

Ty was tossing and turning, like he had been all night. I slipped into my clothes and crept to the kitchen.

I got a shock. There he was. My dad was standing in the kitchen. As if he was waiting for me.

I couldn't look at him.

"'Morning," he said, like it was any ordinary day.

"Hi," I muttered, making myself as busy as I could so I wouldn't have to raise my eyes to his.

"You're up early."

"Yep."

"Brought you a jelly doughnut," he said, holding out a bag with "Winchell's Doughnuts" written on it.

Jelly doughnuts are my favorite.

"Darren says we shouldn't eat junk food," I said, pouring hot water into the oatmeal and stirring it.

He threw the bag down on the counter. "Then I'll make some eggs," he said trying to sound cheerful.

"No time," I said, which was sort of a lie, but not really. I didn't have time — for him.

"Where you going so early?" he asked.

"Same place as usual," I answered grudgingly.

"You gonna keep up this running after school starts?"

"Yep."

"How's your mom feel about that?"

"Fine."

I slurped up the oatmeal as fast as I could, almost choking on it.

"Kisha," he said slowly. He started to make a move toward me. I didn't actually see him, but I could feel it. Then he changed his mind and sat down on one of the stools.

I still wasn't looking at him, but I could see him out of the corner of my eye. His shoulders were all slumped over. His head was in his hands, and he was leaning on the counter. I could have felt sorry for him — under other circumstances. If he'd have hit me, it wouldn't have been so bad.

"Kisha — " He tried again.

I wasn't going to give him any help.

He straightened his shoulders and whirled around toward me. It gave me a fright.

"I'm not going to hurt you, Kisha," he said with this sad kind of voice.

It was pathetic. Like I had no reason to suspect he might hurt me — or anyone else. I didn't say anything. I was scraping the bottom of the bowl, so I'd have someplace to look until I could escape.

"Look at me, Kisha."

I shook my head.

"Please."

"I can't."

"Kisha — what happened yesterday — "

"I don't want to talk about it," I said, getting up as fast as I could.

"We have to talk about it," he said, but I was already halfway out the door.

I glanced up at him as I turned to close it after me. He was just standing there in the doorway to the kitchen.

I closed the door as quickly as I could, but I couldn't get the picture of him out of my mind. He looked as if he was going to crumple up at any minute, and I didn't want to see that. I knew the only thing left would be his eyes. But I also knew that even if I never saw him again, I'd never forget the way he looked at me.

Yesterday I hated him. I still hated him when I woke up this morning. There were lots of times I hated him. I wanted to hate him right now. I didn't want to forget that he had slapped my mother hard enough to leave a handprint on her face. She hadn't done anything that gave him the right to do that. I know. Because I'm pretty sure what she did do that caused him to lose it.

When I had walked to the the mailbox to mail my mother's letter, I looked at the envelope. It was addressed to the Oakland Board of Education.

I put two and two together. Her looking for her high school diploma, their arguing about her getting a job, her always saying she wanted to be a teacher. I knew she couldn't be a real teacher because she'd never gone to college, but she could be a teacher's aid. That's what the argument was all about, I had decided.

I told Tyrone what I thought, and he agreed with me. Neither of us could understand why that would drive my dad crazy. Of course, we knew that he didn't want her to get a job, but it was her life, wasn't it?

Maybe she'd be better off without him, like most of the other mothers at the project. Most of them lived by themselves, just with their kids. Some of their husbands were in jail. Some of them had just walked off one day and never come back. Some of them didn't even have husbands in the first place. Lots of them. They didn't seem to mind so much. Whitman was like a whole city without men, only my dad and the Barton twins' dad. They were the only two men I knew who actually lived here on a regular basis. The rest were just boys.

I felt worse than ever when I rounded the corner to the community center. Why couldn't all men be like Darren? Maybe he *wasn't* married to Lureen but at least he was living with her.

"Hi, Kisha," someone said, startling me back to reality.

It was September, a girl from the project I used to know. She was carrying the cutest little baby.

"What's its name?" I asked, reaching over to pat the baby's hand.

"Clytee."

"Clytee's a nice name. How old is she?"

"Eight months."

"Big, isn't she?"

"So so."

"Cute though. She's real cute."

"Yeah, I think so," September said, but I wasn't so sure about that. Looked to me like she was probably stuck baby-sitting, and cute as that baby was, it was still a baby.

"So where you headed to?" she asked.

"I'm on a track team at the community center," I explained. "You ought to join. You'd be great. Didn't you used to run at school? In seventh grade?"

I was getting excited. September would be a real asset to the team.

"Yeah," she said. "I used to run."

"So, see if your mom can get one of the other kids to sit and come on down."

"I can't," September said.

"How come?"

"The baby."

"Girl, that baby has at least four or five other sisters that can care for her. This is important."

"This baby has no one else to take care of her," September said. "She's *my* baby."

My mouth dropped open, and I stared at September like she'd just dropped down from another planet. *"Your* baby?" I stammered.

"We have our own place," September said proudly. "With my oldest sister and her baby. If you have a baby you can put in for your own apartment. I have my own bedroom. Just me and Clytee. I don't have to share it with six other kids. It's really great. And quiet. Sometimes it's hard to get used to the quiet, but if it gets too lonely, I just go on over to my mom's."

"That's great," I said, swallowing hard.

"And she's a good baby — as babies go."

"You must be real proud of her," I said, embarrassed.

"I *am* proud of her," September said, and she picked up her head, straightened her shoulders, smiled at Clytee, and held her close.

"So, I'll see you around," I said nervously. "I gotta run."

"See you around."

Boy, I thought as I walked away, *I could never do that.* As much as I hated school sometimes, I couldn't imagine not going.

Then all of a sudden it hit me. September is a year older than I am. She's fourteen. Somewhere in the back of my mind I remembered that my mother was fourteen when she had me. It was something she didn't like to talk about. It just sort of slipped out one day.

Not that it was something people at Whitman looked down on. It's just that my mother didn't feel so good about it, and I knew she'd be very upset if I got pregnant at fourteen.

The very thought made me laugh. Me pregnant at fourteen. I'd never even kissed a boy. Never even wanted to. Except Darren, maybe.

But the thought of my mom carrying me around when she was fourteen really got to me.

I know she lived with my grandmother at the time I

was born, and my grandmother took care of me while my mom went to high school, but still, it must have been really weird. She didn't marry my dad and move into her own place until right before Ty was born.

Suddenly, something else hit me. Was that man who hit my mother really my father? I knew he was Tyrone's father. But who said he was mine?

I tried to remember him playing with me when I was a little baby, but I couldn't. I could remember when Ty was born, though. I could remember the actual day.

My dad — if he is my dad — was so happy. I was four years old at the time, and I sort of remember my mom being kind of fat, and all. But no one ever said why. I mean no one told me that she was going to have a baby. It was never discussed, as far as I remember, so it came as a big shock to me.

She was painting this little rocking chair for my room, when she suddenly put down the brush and got this strange look on her face. She called to my dad that it was time. *Time for what?* I wondered. And my dad rushed in from the other room. He called over to my grandmother's house, and she came running. And there was a lot of commotion for a few minutes, and no one paid any attention to me. But I remember feeling scared.

If they'd have told me why everyone was running around, I wouldn't have been so scared, but I didn't know anything, and, of course, not knowing is the worst.

But even worse than that was after my mom and dad ran out of the house, hardly saying good-bye to me, and things calmed down. I started to cry, and my grandmother said to me, sort of irritated, "Don't cry, Kisha. You're a big girl now. You're not the baby no more."

And that was it. That was all she said. Then she got breathless, cooking and cleaning, and left me entirely on my own for hours, just hunched in the corner of the living room.

Finally, the phone rang, and she started screaming, "It's a boy! It's a boy!" Then she remembered I was in the house, and she ran into the living room screaming, "Your mama had a little boy."

Of course, I was old enough to know what that meant.

"When's she coming home?" I asked.

"Two days. Isn't that wonderful? A little boy."

I stared at her.

"Shame on you," she said, giving me a shake. "Jealous of a little baby."

I stuck my thumb in my mouth, something I hadn't done in a long time, and I slouched off to my room.

I remember just lying on my bed thinking nothing was ever going to be the same again, thinking that my little world was falling apart, that from now on, no one would care about what happened to me. All they cared about was that little boy that was coming home with my mom.

Then my dad came in, picked me up, and twirled me around, saying, "That little baby is the luckiest little baby in the world 'cause he has you for a sister."

And he hugged me and hugged me and told me my mom was so worried about taking care of the baby, but he told her he knew they could count on me, that I'd help her out, and I promised I would.

I could laugh thinking about it now. I was so serious. Because he was serious. And when they brought Ty home, first thing my dad did was take him from my mom. He was crying. And my dad put that baby in my arms. I was sitting on my little rocker, which he had finished painting for me. And I held that baby boy, and rocked him, and just like that he stopped crying. And my dad said, "See, I knew Kisha would be a big help."

So — what can I do? I wondered. I guess he *is* my dad. Even if I sometimes wish he weren't.

11

*F*or the next few days everything was quiet around our house. I don't know what went down between my mom and dad, but they had obviously settled on some kind of truce.

Last night, right out of the blue, while we were eating dinner, she announced that she would be walking to school with Ty in the morning. Ty, of course, said she didn't need to. All the kids would rag on a fourth grader coming to school with his mother. But she just laughed and said she was coming to school because she had a job there.

I about dropped dead with shock. She had said it just as calm as can be, and my father was sitting right there. I looked at him out of the corner of my eye. But he was staring straight ahead. I couldn't be sure if he heard what she said, or not. He didn't react. He didn't even move. It was like he'd turned to stone. He didn't look mad, or anything. He just looked blank.

Ty and I didn't know what to say. Given the fact that we had figured out that my dad had gotten himself so worked up about her *applying* for the job, we weren't sure how he'd react now that she'd actually gotten it.

But he didn't react at all. So we just mumbled, "That's nice," or something like that. I guess we felt that if we didn't make too big a deal about it, it might pass right by him, and he'd just stay cool.

Still, I was kind of glad I had to leave early in order to get over to the center by six-thirty so we could work out before school. Though I hated to leave Ty at home by himself — just in case.

As soon as I spotted the center, I relaxed. I couldn't wait to see my friends. We've become so tight. We all get along. We have nicknames for each other. Natonia's is Fire. Alisha's is Slim. I'm Fingers because I'm always pointing at something. Esther is Specs. The twins are The Twins. Tureena is Flash, and Jennifer is Kitten because she's so shy and silky.

I don't know if she's shy around us because she's white, or if she's that way around white people too. I know that when I'm with white people, which is hardly ever except in school, I act different. It's hard to pinpoint exactly how, but I know I do. So does my mom.

She's always very careful to speak correctly. And she always holds her head a certain way.

When I asked her about it once, she just laughed — but she didn't deny it. Also, I never heard her joke around with white people, and I wondered if maybe that was because they didn't have a sense of humor.

Jennifer doesn't really. Or maybe she does, but she doesn't around us. But we're getting used to her anyway. Last week when we were in the bathroom getting changed, Alisha asked her if she could touch her hair. The rest of us looked at each other like — get real, Alisha. But Jennifer said, "Sure."

"It's like silk," Alisha said.

"Let's see," Esther said.

She touched it like it was gold, or something. "Come here, Kisha," she called to me. Just what I needed to bolster my self-esteem.

But pretty soon we were all taking turns combing Jennifer's hair. Even the twins. Their mom's white, but her hair's almost as coarse as mine.

Since then it hasn't felt so weird having Jennifer on the team, though we still don't know how she really feels about us, or whether her *real* friends are the white kids at her school. And some of us still aren't exactly sure how we really feel about her. Me, I try to take it in stride. Just like a million other things, getting to know a white girl is just one more change in my life. I'm going to miss seeing her in the mornings. Now that school's starting, she'll be working out with her dad beforehand and with us after.

"We're not going to run today," Darren said after we'd done warm-ups and jumping jacks and gotten ourselves totally sweated up. "We're going to have a short meeting instead."

We arranged ourselves on the floor.

"Okay. Listen up," he said seriously. "We don't have a lot of rules around here. We haven't had to. But I think we have to get a few things straight now that school's starting. First of all, good grades. If you're gonna run, you have to work. Not only on the track, but in school. Any girl who goofs off is suspended from the team until she pulls her grades up."

"What you gonna do, check our report cards?" Alisha asked.

"I'm going to do more than that," Darren said.

"What do you mean?" Tureena asked.

"I have an appointment with the principal this afternoon. I'm going to tell him I want to meet with all of your teachers. If there's a problem they can call me."

Alisha's eyes about popped out of her head. "You're going to check up on us?"

"Constantly," Darren said, and he laughed.

What Darren was saying might be called spying in some people's eyes. But most of the team seemed to think there was a fine line between spying and caring.

"But what if we're too stupid to get good grades?" Esther asked, nervously pushing her glasses back on her nose.

"None of you is stupid," Darren said. "And I don't expect all A's. At least not at first."

Everyone groaned. Alisha looked nervous. She was repeating eighth grade. School was not exactly a priority for most of us, but until the track team came along I couldn't tell you exactly what had been.

"Rule number two. No drugs."

He looked at us individually as if he wanted to get that through each of our heads.

"No drugs of any kind. And that includes liquor, beer, whatever."

"We don't do drugs," Esther said softly. "At least I don't. My mother would kill me."

"If the drugs didn't," Darren said. "You can't run and do drugs. Period," he added emphatically.

I sneaked a look at Tureena. I'd never actually seen her do drugs, but judging by her boyfriend, I'd have to say it was pretty likely she was using.

Tureena didn't move a muscle. She didn't say a word.

"Third," Darren continued. "I don't want to see any

of you pregnant. So you know what that means. The best way to make sure you don't get pregnant is no sex."

"Should have taken your own advice, Darren," Tureena said, and she snickered.

The rest of us held our breaths. Darren looked stunned. There was this long silence. A silence so complete you could hear the clock ticking from across the room. "Tick, tick, tick," over and over again.

Then Darren's face relaxed. "Yeah," he said. "You're right. I should have taken a lot of people's advice, but I guess I thought I could get away with it."

"Forget it, Darren. Tureena didn't mean nothing," Natonia said, giving Tureena the evil eye.

"No. No. I can't forget it. Not that I want to. I love Lureen. I love my baby. But neither of us was ready to have a kid, and we're a lot older than you are. We learned what I'm trying to teach you all. But we learned the hard way," Darren said.

Then he got that faraway look in his eyes that he sometimes gets, and he said, "Yeah — I learned the hard way about a lot of things. So I don't want to see any of the guys who hang out at the center sniffing around, you hear? You want to have boyfriends, that's okay, but keep your mind on track and learn how to say no. There's only one way out of the project. You have to work hard and stay clean. If you do well in school — and I'll see that you do — if you keep training, the way you have been, and stay cool about sex, you'll be able to make something of your lives."

Well, it was a good pep talk. The same kind we heard the first day of school every year, the kind that every kid forgets by the second. The kind the teachers forget too.

But, who knows? Maybe Darren did believe in us. Maybe we really could break the cycle. And besides, I'd never had a teacher who admitted she'd done something she wished she hadn't.

"I'm sorry we don't have showers in the community center," Darren said. "That's something I'm planning on getting in the future. For the time being, you'll have to wash up in the bathroom before school. I made sure there would be plenty of paper towels in there."

Natonia and I walked off together. Everyone was complaining about being all sweaty. Most of us had brought a change of clothes in a paper bag, but we were soaked through to our underwear.

We took turns washing up. It was kind of embarrassing after Darren's talk about sex and stuff, but we started horsing around, pinching each other on the butt and giggling. Then Tureena sauntered over to the mirror and put on her lipstick. We all watched.

"Any of you virgins want to borrow it?" she offered.

"Me!" we all shouted.

One by one we transformed ourselves. We all screamed as soon as one of us finished and passed the lipstick to the next in line. Then — after all the commotion — there was this hush. We stood and looked at ourselves in the mirror. Our red lips were smiling, but our eyes were serious. We knew that somehow over the past few weeks we had become more than just a team.

"Get a move on," Darren called from downstairs.

We finished washing up, and out of the corner of my eye I saw that Natonia had really blossomed. She wore her uncles' big old shirts all summer, so I hadn't noticed before, but when she took off her shirt, I could see her puffing up out of her bra.

"Stop staring at me, girl," Natonia said.

"I wasn't staring," I lied.

I got busy washing up myself.

Despite the fact that money was scarce, we looked pretty sharp. Somehow our mothers had scraped together enough money so we could look nice this first day of school, at least.

We rushed down the stairs past Darren and headed to school together like one big family.

■ ■ ■

Just as Natonia, Esther and I were about to sit down in English class first period, this stupid-looking boy named Henry that I remembered from last year, pretended to "accidentally" bump into Natonia. Then he got right up next to her so they were squeezed in between the desks, and he whispered something to her. She froze for a second, then she raised her hand and hauled off and punched him smack in the face.

Everyone was shocked. Especially Ms. Collins, the new English teacher.

Nobody moved. Including Henry.

Finally Henry put his hand up to his face and spit at Natonia.

By that time Ms. Collins had recovered from her shock and was standing beside them.

"Both of you see me after class," she said pretty calmly, given what had just gone on. "For the time being, please sit down."

Natonia breathed fire at her and continued standing. Henry crossed to the opposite side of the room.

"He deserved it," Natonia said. "He touch me again, or say that to me again, I'll kick him in the — "

"Sit down," Ms. Collins commanded.

"I will," Natonia said.

I wasn't sure if the "I will" meant she'd kick Henry's butt, or she'd sit down.

She sat down. It probably meant both things.

I could see that Ms. Collins was a little shaken up. She was breathing hard as she walked back to her desk, but she smiled at us and said, "Well, I can see this is going to be an exciting class. I'm not sure I can compete with the drama we've already had, but I'm going to try."

I had to give her credit for honesty. Most teachers would try to go right on as if nothing had happened while everyone would still be thinking about what had gone on, not about what the teacher was saying. Maybe Ms. Collins was smarter than our other teachers.

"This is my first year at Martin Luther King Jr. High School," she said, "but it's not my first year of teaching. So while I know a few tricks, I admit I don't know all of them. Some of you can probably get away with not doing your work, but I probably wouldn't try it. And it's true. I do have eyes in the back of my head," she said without cracking a smile. "What I'm hoping, though, is that the class will interest you enough to keep you involved, so you'll want to do the work."

Well, this was definitely a first, I thought.

"We're going to read a book called *Annie John* first thing," she said.

She picked up a paperback book from her desk and showed it to us. It had a picture of a black girl on the cover.

I sat up at my desk. Thank goodness we weren't reading about that stupid *Jane Eyre* again. I hated that book. I couldn't believe anyone could be so afraid to speak up. The woman acted like a slave. I hated it. Natonia really hated it.

"Wait a minute," I said, more to myself than to Ms. Collins.

"Yes?" Ms. Collins said.

She wasn't even pissed at me for interrupting her without raising my hand.

"Sorry," I apologized. "I was just wondering. Is that girl on the cover Annie John?"

"Well, the book isn't an autobiography, but it *is* based on the author's experiences," Ms. Collins explained. "And the author is a black woman. So the drawing on the cover might look something like Jamaica Kincaid did when she was a girl."

"Was she a slave?" I asked.

"No, she wasn't, but that's a good question. A question I'd like to discuss at length one day. I'd like to talk about what it is to be a slave."

"We all know what a slave is," Natonia said.

"Do we?" Ms. Collins asked.

"They were our great-grandparents who were dragged over here from Africa against their will," Monroe Jones said.

"And sold and beaten," Shakur McBee said.

"They couldn't ever make their own choices or decide what they wanted to do with their lives," Natonia said. "Someone always had control over them."

"And what about you?" Ms. Collins asked. "Are you slaves?"

Everyone shouted, "No! Of course not!" And we looked at her like she'd flipped out, or something. What kind of question was that for a black woman to ask?

She just smiled at us — this nice, gentle smile — and said softly. "Well, I'm glad about that."

Then she handed out the books, and we started reading *Annie John* together. Out loud. Which was something we hardly ever did in school anymore. We took turns. Some kids could read better than others. Some kids said they didn't want to read, and that was okay with Ms. Collins. She just went on to the next kid, but even the kids who didn't read were quiet, as if they were listening. The story was pretty interesting. All about Annie John's childhood. But the thing is, we'd also stop and talk about it, and talk about memories from our own childhoods.

It was downright poetic.

When Ms. Collins said we should finish the chapter at home tonight, no one groaned. When the bell rang, none of us wanted to leave.

12

Natonia was still talking about Ms. Collins on the way
to the community center after school.

"I couldn't believe it. I just couldn't believe it," she
kept repeating over and over again. "I expected that
woman to beat my butt, and all she did was ask us
exactly what happened, and before you know it, we
were telling her — the truth. Both of us. I think old
Henry was more scared than I was. But we were both
so surprised that she actually wanted to listen, we just
told her."

I still couldn't get over it. Ms. Collins didn't even
punish them or holler at them. She just told Henry that
Natonia might pay more attention to him if he showed
her some respect. He said he didn't mean to "dis" Natonia, which was a major first for Henry, I was sure. He
disrespected everyone.

"Sounds like Henry likes you," I said, teasing Natonia. "You better watch out, or I'll tell Darren."

"Don't you go telling Darren nothing, girl," Natonia hissed at me.

I jumped back. "I was kidding."

"Well, don't kid," she snapped. "I'm not in the mood."

There she was going off on me again, right out of the blue. One minute ago, she was all happy that Ms. Collins had listened to her, and the next she couldn't even take a little joke.

Natonia hugged her books close to her and marched on ahead — which was okay with me. I was getting a little tired of her famous moods, anyway.

I took my time, and when I got there most of the other girls had already changed back into their workout clothes. They were just hanging around, waiting for Darren, who was in his office talking on the phone. I could see him through the glass door. He smiled and waved. I waved back. But I didn't feel much like smiling. Natonia's cranky mood was enough to put me in one, too.

I changed into my sweats, folded my school clothes up nice, and ran back to the main room. As I came in, I heard Esther ask Natonia, "Where's Tureena at?"

"Why're you looking at me?" Natonia said. "I don't know where she is."

"Well, excuse *me*," Esther said, moving away from Natonia.

I went over and sat down next to Esther.

When Darren came out of his office, he asked the same question.

We all shrugged our shoulders and took pains not to look at Natonia. Nobody wanted to set her off again.

"Anybody see her in school?" Darren asked.

Nobody had, which was kind of strange. She'd walked to school with the rest of us this morning.

I looked around. We were all here except Tureena. Jennifer had come in with her father a few minutes earlier and was sitting on the floor next to Alisha.

"Okay," Darren said. "Unless Tureena has some good excuse for not being here, she's off the team. She knows the rules."

"Come on," Natonia said, all irritated. "We get more than one chance, don't we?"

"Sometimes in life, you only get one chance," Darren said kind of sadly.

"Tureena sometimes has problems following rules, but she's the best relay runner we have," Esther said. "Give her another chance."

"Come on, Darren," we all shouted. Even Jennifer. "It would be bad for the team."

"Let me go get her," Alisha said, jumping up before Darren could answer. "I think I know where she is."

"Okay," Darren agreed, "but if you can't find her right away, come on back. You have work to do if you want to grab onto that ring. Someone want to go with Alisha?" Darren asked.

"Me," I said, raising my hand.

Of course, I didn't really want to go, but I wanted Darren to see that I was responsible, the kind of person you could depend on, like a grown-up. Well, like some grown-ups.

I followed Alisha out of the community center. She wasn't exactly the type to volunteer. But she was probably doing it for Tureena, who was her best friend. They both have the same kind of sad look in their eyes even when they're laughing. Like no matter how good it got, there was still something at the back of their minds telling them to watch out. Because next thing you know something terrible was going to happen, like failing a test, or losing your wallet, which was probably empty anyway, or getting your lunch money stolen from you at school, which happened regularly, or your mother getting beat up, or your father losing his job — if you had a father.

Alisha and Tureena seemed to understand each other, protect each other. I wondered if I still had a best friend. Or if I still wanted Natonia to be my best friend. I wondered if Natonia would come look for me if I didn't show up for practice. Probably not. But Esther would. Or the twins. I knew I'd go look for Natonia, though, even if I was mad at her. And not only because she was such a good long-distance runner.

The one big difference between Alisha and Tureena was their looks. I hate to say it, but Alisha was all scrawny and gangly. Tureena was gorgeous, though. Really gorgeous. Like movie-star gorgeous. And she knew it, too. Not that she was stuck on herself. She wasn't. But she knew people looked at her when she walked down the street, and she even walked like a movie star.

I didn't know that much about Tureena outside the team, except what I'd heard from Natonia. All I knew was that her mom was in jail for dealing, or using, or something, and who knew where her dad was. Nobody around here, that was for sure. Tureena was living with her seventeen-year-old sister, who already had two kids. And there was Tureena's gangster boyfriend, Jaguar. But when we were in training, it was like she wasn't any different from the rest of us. Of course, we were all different in our ways, but having one goal somehow put us in the same box. One that was big enough to contain our differences.

I'd been thinking so hard I hadn't really noticed where we were walking until we got there.

"Oh no," I said. "Not here."

"Don't worry," Alisha said. "I know my way around. They trust me."

I made a "V" with my two fingers and started cursing myself for trying to impress Darren. I tried to hide behind Alisha, which was impossible, but I refused to stand next to her when she went right up to the crack house and knocked on the door.

I was shaking. If my mom saw me standing here, she'd go crazy.

A mean-looking guy with a diamond stud in his nose stuck his head out. I almost fainted. It was the same guy Darren had wrestled to the ground.

What was I doing here?

"I need to talk to Tureena," Alisha said.

The guy closed the door in our faces.

"Let's go," I whispered, pulling on Alisha's sleeve. "She's obviously not here."

"Yes, she is," Alisha assured me.

Before I could say another word, Tureena opened the door and slipped out. She motioned for us to walk away from the house, which was fine with me.

"Darren's waiting for you," Alisha said.

"Tell him I can't come," Tureena said.

"You better, Tureena," Alisha said, staring her down.

"Jaguar says he doesn't want me on the team."

"You weren't in school this afternoon," Alisha said.

"I came over here during lunch," Tureena said, as if that was some kind of explanation.

"I know you did, but you said you were just gonna stay a minute."

"Jaguar didn't want me to leave."

"You gonna let that homeboy tell you what to do?" Alisha asked.

I was standing there, feeling proud of Alisha. She never had the nerve to talk like that before she joined the track team.

"He gave me this," Tureen said, holding out her hand.

She was sporting this ring. Probably a diamond, or something. It sparkled in the sun, and it was huge, like you see on TV in those ads.

"Well, you can just give it back," Alisha said. "You know what that means."

"I can't give it back," Tureena said.

"Yes, you can!" Alisha shouted.

"Shush," I said, looking toward the door.

Alisha moved closer to Tureena and lowered her voice.

"We got a chance with Darren. Even you know that," Alisha said emphatically. "Right now it's our only chance to get out of here. You want to spend the rest of your life in this hellhole like your sister. Or in jail like your mama?"

"Don't believe everything you hear," Tureena said. "Darren can't get us out of here."

"That's right," I said, moved to defend Darren. "You got to get your*self* out, but he can help you. You give up going to school, give up being on the track team, spend your time hanging out with guys like Jaguar, you're never going to get out."

"You hang around with Jaguar, eventually you're dead meat," Alisha said.

"It's too late," Tureena said.

I could see she was trying to keep from crying. She put her hand up to her right eye and sort of wiped a tear away. Made me feel so bad I wanted to cry right with her.

"It's not too late," Alisha said.

"You heard what Darren said this morning," Tureena whispered. "He wouldn't want me on the team."

I knew what she meant, and so did Alisha. But I also knew Darren. He wouldn't punish anyone for fooling around before he told us not to. And he didn't actually say not to, he just warned us not to get pregnant. Anybody would have done the same thing. You couldn't hardly be expected to run track if you were carrying a baby.

I explained all this to Tureena and tried to convince her to come back to the center to practice. It was the most I'd ever said to her at one time. I sort of got carried away with my mission.

It didn't do much good, though. I thought I'd been pretty convincing, but she had obviously made up her mind, and there was nothing I could say that would change it.

She'd made a choice. Or, at least, she'd let someone make it for her. As far as I was concerned, it was the wrong choice.

But all the stuff Alisha was saying about getting out of Whitman kind of stuck in my mind.

Everyone I knew lived at Whitman except for Esther and Jennifer. My grandmother lived here, even my great-grandmother. My mother. Two of my uncles. I'd heard what Darren had said, but I hadn't really taken it in. It had never really occurred to me before that there was a choice. We just lived here. And it didn't seem all that bad, if you stayed out of the wrong places and kept to yourself. I couldn't even imagine living anyplace else.

But Alisha had obviously been thinking about it hard. She wanted out. I could see that.

But what did that mean? Where was out, and what would we do when and if we got there?

When we walked back into the community center, the other girls were already warming up. They all stopped and looked from Alisha to me and back to Alisha again, silently asking the same question. Darren walked over to us.

"Did you find her?"

"No," Alisha said quickly.

Without batting an eye, I backed her up.

13

After a while we all stopped asking Alisha about Tureena, but that didn't mean we stopped thinking about her. We missed her sassy attitude. We missed *her.* But worrying about what might happen to her sort of brought the rest of us even closer together.

Lots of times we'd talk on the phone all night, do our homework together.

I was surprised. So were the other kids. Most of us did a lot better on our report cards than we'd done since kindergarten. I got two A's, which made my mother totally happy. The C in biology didn't please her all that much, but I was trying to bring up my grade.

Natonia, much to her surprise, but not mine, turned out to be real smart. I was a little jealous. I worked like a dog for my grades. Well, not exactly that hard, but I had to study. It sort of came naturally to her, once she sat down and decided to do it.

But lately, her grades had been going down. I heard Ms. Collins talking to her about them yesterday. She was real quiet, but I caught a word here and there. Natonia didn't say anything to me about it, but I knew it bothered her.

It seemed to affect the way she ran, too. She wasn't herself after school.

She wasn't in school at all one day. And I was thinking about stopping over at her place after practice, if it wasn't dark yet, but when I walked into the center, there she was, looking a little peaked, but ready to go.

By the time I changed into my workout clothes, I didn't have much time to talk to her — just "hi," "how come you weren't in school?" and stuff. She said she'd accidentally slept in, but I had this funny feeling inside. Like something was wrong. Like maybe she was trying to tell me something, only I had earplugs in my ears, so I could only hear muffled sounds.

I kept looking over at her, but I couldn't catch her eye, even though I knew she was looking over at me when I wasn't looking at her.

"Okay," Darren yelled. "Let's get over to the track."

We all piled into Darren's and Jennifer's father's cars. Half of us sitting on top of the other half, making jokes, the way we always did. Only Natonia was really quiet, which led me to believe I was right about something's being wrong. Usually, she had the loudest mouth in the group.

"You feeling okay?" I asked her when we got to the track.

"I'm fine," she whispered.

We walked past a lunch truck in the parking lot. The smells of burritos and hamburgers made me feel faint. I could have eaten a cow, but Darren said it wasn't good to eat heavy foods before we ran, so I just inhaled and dreamed about eating instead.

We lined up, got our usual pep talk about starting slowly, keeping it nice and steady, lifting our legs as high as we could. Then Darren blew his whistle and sang out, "Once around the track to begin with."

We flew. I could feel Natonia beside me, straining more than usual. Usually, we ran neck and neck for about four seconds, then she sprinted out ahead of everybody. I had gotten a lot better. I wasn't always the last one. My feet had started to obey my head, and I didn't trip over them anymore, but I could never keep up with Natonia, so I was surprised when she stayed at my speed and even more surprised when she fell behind me. I would have turned to look, but that was one of Darren's rules. No looking back.

I slowed down a little, waiting for Natonia to whiz past me, but I couldn't feel her presence in back of me. I slowed down even more. My heart began to beat fast. But not from running hard.

We were almost around the track. My stomach was in knots.

"Timings's off," Darren said as he clocked me. Except for Natonia, I was the last one in. My being last wasn't unusual, but her being last was. She was almost always first.

She seemed to be wobbling as she took the last few feet of the track.

Without thinking, I broke away from Darren and ran over to her. She lunged forward and fell into my arms.

"Darren! Darren!" I cried as Natonia and I tumbled to the ground.

He came running over and kneeled down beside her.

"She fainted," he said.

He called her name.

"Oh my God," I said.

The other girls gathered around.

"Let's give her some air," Darren said softly. "She's gonna be all right." He called her name again.

Slowly Natonia opened her eyes. She blinked, then she closed them again as if it was just too painful to look at the world.

"She gonna be all right?" I asked Darren.

"I'm hungry," Natonia said, opening her eyes again.

"When was the last time you ate?" Darren asked her.

"Yesterday," she said.

"When yesterday?"

"Morning," she whispered. "A Winchell's doughnut."

"Stay here," Darren said.

He put his sweatshirt under her head and his jacket over her, then he ran off.

"You okay? You okay?" I kept asking Natonia. I sat down beside her and took her hand.

She nodded her head weakly.

Esther kneeled down and straightened out the jacket so it covered her arms. Jennifer sat down and patted Natonia's other hand.

A few minutes later Darren came back carrying two burgers and a pint of milk.

"Try to eat this slowly," he said, helping Natonia sit up.

She tried eating slowly — for about two minutes, then she wolfed down both burgers and gulped down the milk.

"Yesterday?" Darren asked.

"Maybe the day before," she said. "I didn't have time to go over to the main market, and Mr. Abrakus won't let me in his store."

"Because of what happened with the cans?" I asked.

She nodded her head yes.

"I have to drop off the team," she mumbled without looking at Darren or me.

"You can't," I said. "You're the best runner."

"What's going on?" Darren asked. "How come you're not eating regularly?"

"I told you, with being here in the morning and after school, I don't have time to go to the store."

"What happened to your grandmother?" he asked.

"Nothing."

"Nothing you want to talk about, you mean," he said gently.

"Yeah," she said. "Nothing I want to talk about."

She said it kind of nasty, but I knew she didn't mean it that way.

"We'll figure something out," Darren said, as he helped her up from the ground. "Let me get the other girls back on the track first."

None of us felt like running, of course, but we could hardly say that. We all wanted to hear what was going on. But we ran around the track four more times, anyway, did leaps, ran the stairs, and finally piled back into the cars so tired we could hardly talk.

I don't know what Natonia told Darren, but whatever it was, she looked like she wasn't about to tell me, and I knew enough not to push her.

"I'll walk you home," I said to Natonia when we got back to the center. I knew she didn't like me to, but I thought maybe she'd change her mind today, given that she'd fainted, and all.

She didn't resist this time. We walked over to her place. We just stood around for a few minutes. I kept hoping her grandmother would open the door, and I'd smell something cooking inside, but she didn't. And Natonia didn't go into the house, either. Maybe they'd had a fight, and Natonia was afraid to go in. Though I couldn't picture Natonia being afraid of anyone, especially her grandmother.

"It's getting dark," she said finally.

"Yeah," I said, hating to walk away.

"You better go."

"Yeah, I better."

I just stood there like a fool.

"Yeah," she repeated.

"See you."

"See you."

I started to walk away. "Will you be in school tomorrow?"

"Yeah. I guess so."

"Okay. So see you."

I waved at her and walked away feeling defeated, without knowing exactly why. All I knew was that if I'd asked the right questions, I'd have gotten some answers, but I didn't know what the right questions were.

It was weird when you thought about it. You know someone practically all your life, then you don't know them anymore. You practically live with someone. You do the same things, go to the same school, have private jokes, even get your periods together, then one day it turns out you're almost strangers.

One thing can happen, and they're different. Or maybe you're different.

It hadn't happened all at once, but it had happened. And it made me sad. I don't like things to change even if they change for the good. But when they change for the bad, it really stings. And sometimes, it was hard to tell if it was good or bad.

Even my family life had changed. My mother still looked at my school papers and asked me all kinds of questions. Tyrone still watched the news on TV all the time. My father was still out of work. But things were different. My mom went to school every day. She was a teacher's aid for first grade. She loved it. She had all kinds of stories to tell when we ate dinner. She was happy, and she talked a lot more than she ever had before. I was happy for her. So was Ty. But my dad got quieter and quieter. Sometimes he didn't say a word. He just drank.

14

I thought about it a long time, and I decided that even though we were all part of a team, Natonia was still my best friend. I had to give her the opportunity to talk to me even if she didn't know she wanted to.

The next morning, I left early enough to stop by for her on the way to the center. But standing in front of her door, I felt kind of weird. I should have called first. But it was too late now. I'd already knocked.

"Well, if it isn't Kisha," her grandmother said when she opened the door. "You want some breakfast?"

"Sure," I said, walking into the house. I realized I'd left without eating. I was starving.

Natonia's grandmother didn't seem mad at her, or anyone else.

"I made some pancake batter for the boys," she said giving the big bowl on the counter a stir.

"I love your pancakes."

She put some oil in a pan, lit the stove, then plopped four big spoonfuls of batter in. Two for me and two for Natonia.

Strangely enough, though, she put all the pancakes on one plate when they were ready. And she put out one napkin and one fork.

"Ms. Washington — ," I said softly.

"You like those pancakes? Eat 'em while they're hot."

"I love them," I said, but good as they were I was having trouble getting them down for some reason.

"Ms. Washington," I said, trying again.

"Lordy, it was cold last night," Ms. Washington said as she looked out of the window.

"Yeah, it was," I said.

I heard some noise from the back room. Maybe Natonia was still getting dressed.

"Those boys of mine are the laziest things. Look at that. Seven o'clock, and they're just getting to bed. Won't be up till after noon."

"Seven o'clock," I repeated, starting to panic about the time.

"You better be getting over to the community center."

"But — "

"Don't bother about cleaning up your dishes. I'll take care of that."

"Ms. Washington — "

"Hurry on. Darren doesn't like you girls to be late."

Before I knew it I was standing in front of the house, and Ms. Washington had closed the door.

I kicked the side of the curb and walked over to the center.

Natonia was standing in the doorway, jumping up and down to keep warm, waiting for Darren to show up with the key.

"You're early," I said.

"Yeah, finished breakfast and ran over," she said.

"What'd you eat?"

"Toast, grits, some eggs, milk."

"Big breakfast. You must be feeling better."

"Lots."

"You make it?"

"Make what?"

"Your breakfast."

"My grandmother did."

"That so?"

"She always makes breakfast."

"She made you something special this morning."

"Nah. She always makes the same thing. Toast, grits, eggs."

"She made pancakes today."

"Oh yeah, and how do you know that?" Natonia asked sarcastically, but at the same time, she had this funny, almost terrified, look on her face.

"I don't know," I said, looking away from her. "Just guessed."

At that moment, Darren came whizzing around the corner into his parking space, and all the other girls came running in from different directions.

"Winter's on the way," Darren shouted as he unlocked the door.

"Let's run inside today," Esther suggested.

"We'll work out inside this morning. Then run the track as usual after school. It'll be warmer then."

I watched Natonia carefully as we exercised. She looked okay. Maybe not great. But okay.

By the time we reached our English class, I couldn't stand it anymore. "I was at your house this morning," I whispered. "You didn't have no grits and eggs for breakfast."

Natonia didn't say a word. She just stared straight ahead, like she hadn't heard what I said.

We were both relieved when Ms. Collins whipped into the room and started asking questions before she even got to her desk. By the time she took roll we were already involved in the discussion for the day.

Before we knew it, we were talking about slavery again. We were reading this essay written by some poor woman explaining about how hard it was to keep clean without having the money to buy soap and how difficult it was to send your kids off to school without money to buy shoes.

We could all relate to that, of course. I couldn't really relate to the clean part since my mother would rather starve than leave a dish unwashed or a piece of clothing dirty, but maybe we had more money than this woman did.

Anyway, Ms. Collins was saying how a person didn't have to literally be a slave to be one, and that this woman was a slave to poverty because she couldn't get out of the system. She had no education so she couldn't get a job, and without a job she couldn't get an education because she couldn't pay for it, and even if she did get a job, who would take care of the kids she had?

Well, we could understand that. It's just that we'd never thought about it before. Ms. Collins said people were slaves to all kinds of things. Some people were slaves to drugs. Anytime you were forced to do what someone or something made you do, you were a slave. Then she asked if any of us could think of an example of someone who was a slave.

Henry said his brother was a slave to alcohol. One day when he was eight or nine, someone gave him a beer, and that was it. From that day on, all his brother thought about was drinking. He'd stop, but not for long, and all it took was one little drink to get him started again.

Ms. Collins said that was a good example. We talked about Henry's brother some more, then all of a sudden Natonia says, "Sometimes a person becomes a slave because they're scared, but then they realize they'd rather die than have to do what they hate."

"That's exactly right," Ms. Collins said. "Any of you know this spiritual we sing in my church, 'Before I'd be a slave I'd be buried in my grave'?" she asked.

She started to sing, and some of us joined in with her, just singing along right in class. And for the first time we really understood that song.

When we finished singing, Ms. Collins asked Natonia if she wanted to give a specific example of what she had said. She always liked people to give examples to prove their points. But Natonia said, no, she was just making a statement, and Ms. Collins was totally cool and let it go at that.

I stuck close to Natonia all day. At lunch I offered her half of my sandwich, even though I was starving, be-

cause she said she'd forgotten hers. She took it. I wished
I had some money to buy something else, but I didn't.

After school, we headed for the community center.
When we got about halfway there, Natonia said, "I
can't be no slave no more."

I held my breath and waited for her to say something
else.

"I can't live at my grandmother's house."

"Because she won't let you?" I burst out, remember-
ing how nice her grandmother had been to me just this
morning.

"She'll let me," Natonia said, "but the price is too
high."

"Just tell me where you're living?" I asked quietly.

She rolled her eyes, like if I was too stupid not to
know that, I was too stupid to talk to. She was obviously
living on the street. I knew that. Why'd I have to ask?

"Come to my house," I said quickly. "You can sleep
with me and Ty."

"Maybe," she said. "And maybe not."

I almost burst with joy. She'd opened the door a crack
and let me in. I knew she'd come to my house after
practice.

I didn't push her. I just asked if she wanted to walk
me home.

"Maybe I will," she said, like she was doing me a
favor, and in a way she was.

My mother was cooking tomato sauce when we walked in the door. Natonia trailed into the kitchen after me and stood behind me. "Natonia's having dinner with us," I said, like I had a million times in the past. I knew it would be no big deal.

"That's fine," my mother said.

"And I invited her to sleep over," I said, trying to sound casual about it.

"You know the rules about sleeping over on a school night."

"I know," I said, "but this is an emergency." I tried to signal my mother with my eyes that I would tell her about it later.

"What kind of emergency?" she asked lightly, like she thought I was kidding.

"A private emergency," I said.

"You know you two don't get your sleep when Natonia's here," my mother said.

I could have killed her. Why did she have to go on like this?

"Mom!" I wailed.

Natonia was pulling on my sleeve. I was totally humiliated. I felt like a slave to my mother's stupid rules.

"I'm gonna go," Natonia said.

"No!" I cried. "If you go, I'm going with you."

Suddenly, my mother got the picture. She looked at both of us for a minute, then she said softly, "Every rule has an exception. You stay here as long as you like, Natonia."

Before I could even say thanks, we heard this roar from the living room, and my dad comes stomping into the kitchen like a crazy person.

"This is not a hotel!" he shouted at us.

We all just stood there, too surprised to say anything.

"I said Natonia could stay," my mother hissed.

It was the first time I'd ever actually seen her stand up to my dad in public.

"Well, I say she can't," my dad answered back.

Natonia turned to leave.

"Wait!" I screamed.

Natonia continued walking.

"I'm gonna call Darren," I said, rushing over to the phone. "Natonia — wait a minute."

My father brushed past Natonia and slammed out of the kitchen.

"Maybe it would be better if you did call Darren," my mother said nervously.

"You can be a slave in your own house," I muttered under my breath as I dialed Darren's number.

I didn't say much over the phone, just that me and Natonia had to talk to him right away.

He said he'd just walked in the door. Could it wait?

"No," I said. "It can't."

I stood outside with Natonia even though we were both freezing. Somehow I couldn't look at either of my parents, but I was even more angry with my mother than I was with my father. Because she knew better.

Natonia let me do the talking, and for once I didn't say too much. I just told him that Natonia didn't have a place to sleep. Period.

"Sure, she does," Darren said. "At my house."

Natonia sucked her breath in, then let it out very slowly.

"What about your family?"

"They love company," he said.

I know he didn't mean it that way, but I felt like what he said was a direct blow to me personally. Like maybe his family loved company, but my family didn't.

Darren went around and opened the door for Natonia. She got in. Then he walked around to the driver's side and got in himself.

"See you tomorrow," he said. He winked at me.

I didn't care. What did it mean, anyway? Natonia drove off without even saying good-bye to me.

15

Now that Natonia was part of a new family, it seemed like she was in a better mood. If she wanted to hang out with them, it was fine with me. I didn't care all that much anymore, anyway. I had other friends. Me and Esther liked to hang out together sometimes, though she always seemed to have an endless amount of chores to do, given the fact that there were all those kids in her family.

But none of us are gonna have time to hang out together anymore, what with the big meet coming up. This is what we'd been planning for since summer. We'd been begging and begging Darren to let us compete, but he said he was holding us back until we were good and ready. He didn't want to tip his hat too soon. So we sat out the first meet and the second; then suddenly, he said we were ready.

We couldn't believe we were actually going out of town, down to Los Angeles, to compete against all the other junior high schools in our district. We'd been dying to see how we compared with other kids.

Darren borrowed an old van from someone, so we wouldn't have to sit on top of each other the whole seven or eight hours, or however long it took to get to L.A., and we were totally stoked. We'd be leaving really early Saturday morning. The meet was Saturday afternoon.

Only one thing, we didn't have matching outfits, so even though we felt like a team, we didn't look much like one. That was kind of too bad, but there wasn't much we could do about it. None of us, except Jennifer maybe, could afford an extra pair of shorts and a T-shirt. Hell, we were still trying to save for track shoes. We were pooling our money until we had enough to buy shoes for all of us at the same time.

We'd had a couple of bake sales and a dance at the center and raised some money, but not enough. A weird thing happened though. Alisha's older brother — who everybody called Mean Millard and who also lived in the project, but not with Alisha and her mother — came by with a brand-new TV one day and donated it to Darren for a raffle.

We were going out of our minds until Darren told

133

Millard thanks, but no thanks. We about died, but Millard said just as nice as could be, "I understand, man. I was trying to help out. I just wish you'd been around when I was thirteen."

Then he left, and we all jumped on Darren even though we understood why he couldn't accept a stolen article. But Darren said not to worry, we'd get the things we needed.

And that's what happened. Almost. We came to the center on Friday for a short workout, and there was this box right in the middle of the floor.

As soon as we sat down, Darren opened it and started tossing clothes into the air. The local Army/Navy store had donated uniforms, brown tank tops and shorts.

We each grabbed what looked like our size and ran upstairs to the bathroom to change.

When we came down, we pretended to be dancers in a chorus. We looked so hot. We were a team.

"I got one set left," Darren said. "Who's missing?"

"Esther," I said, suddenly realizing she wasn't there. "I'll go call her."

On my way to the phone in Darren's office I wondered if Natonia noticed that I hadn't had to ask for Esther's phone number.

Just as I opened the door, Darren shouted that Esther had come in. He threw her an outfit. Her face fell, and her eyes filled up with tears.

Nobody could figure out what was going on.

"I got to talk to you," Esther said to Darren.

Darren moved across the room with Esther so they could have some privacy.

We all looked at each other. Maybe she got her period and didn't feel like running.

"That's okay. Don't worry," Darren said as he and Esther walked back to the group. "We'll work something out. We're just going to do some stretches and leg pulls, then we'll take care of it."

Here we go again, I thought. *Another orphan.*

We got into our routine, then Darren gave us a pep talk, telling us how good we were and how much we'd already accomplished. Well, I wasn't sure how good we were. We'd never competed against anyone, but I knew we'd come a long, long way since the summer. And I was proud of that. It was as if I'd grown into myself. Finally I fit together. My feet were the right size for the rest of my body.

"Now, don't forget, set your alarms. Be here at five o'clock tomorrow morning. Sharp," he said, "and bring your uniforms."

I loved the sound of that — uniforms.

I was so happy I forgot about Esther's problem until Darren walked up to me as I was leaving.

"Thought you might like to drive over to Esther's house with me," he said.

"What about Natonia?" I asked.

"She's going to do a few things here, then I'll pick her up when I bring you back home."

"How come?" I asked.

"Esther said her mother likes you."

I was glad to hear that Esther's mother liked me, but it was no surprise. Most everyone's mother liked me 'cause I was so polite — or chicken — whichever way you wanted to look at it.

"I meant how come we're going over there."

"I thought you might be able to help Esther with her problem. I'll tell you about it on the way."

Esther was standing by the car when we got there. Darren unlocked it, and I got in the front seat. She got in the back.

"This isn't going to work," Esther said as Darren pulled away.

"Worth a try," Darren said.

"What isn't going to work?" I asked.

"My mother won't let me go tomorrow," Esther said, just like that.

For a minute I thought she was kidding, but a minute later I realized she wasn't.

"How come?"

"It's Saturday."

"So what?"

"It's the Sabbath."

I started to laugh. "Sunday's the Sabbath, fool." I was relieved to have settled the problem so easily.

"Not for us," Esther said quietly.

"Esther, Sunday is the Sabbath for everyone."

"I'm Jewish," Esther said. "We celebrate the Sabbath on Saturday."

Well, you could have knocked me over. I wasn't exactly sure what being Jewish entailed. I mean I wasn't stupid. I'd heard the word. We had several Jewish teachers in school. But they were white. I didn't know what to say.

"So for us the Sabbath begins on Friday night and ends Saturday at sundown. My mom made this big exception allowing me to run on Saturdays, but she said she just couldn't see allowing me to compete with other people on the Lord's day."

I let out a low whistle. What a time to drop this bomb.

"I kept hoping something would happen," Esther explained. "I guess I didn't want to think about it."

"God," I said. "We can't go without you. We can't."

"I know," Esther wailed.

I was afraid if I turned around to look at her she'd start to cry. Hell, I felt like crying myself. What was I supposed to do? So what if her mother liked me. I wasn't Jewish. I didn't know what to say to her. I wasn't any good in situations like this. I hated all the responsibility.

By the time we got to Esther's I'd worked myself up into a nice little sweat. I felt like throwing up.

Darren opened the car door and motioned for me to get out. I all but crawled out of the car and dragged myself up the stairs to Esther's house.

When we walked into the apartment, I was prepared for a battle of sorts, but I wasn't prepared for what I saw. The whole house had been transformed. Not that anything had changed that much, but it looked totally different.

There was a white tablecloth on the table and cloth napkins and two candle holders with white candles in them. A twisted bread on the table and wine. And the house was spotless. It was usually clean, but I mean how clean can it be with all those kids? Everything was absolutely shining now, as if it had been dusted and waxed to death.

I felt like saying Merry Christmas, or something like that, but I knew that wasn't the right thing to say.

Esther's mother came out of the kitchen, and the smells of soup and roast chicken clung to her clothes. Boy, I sure could have used a chicken leg. I was starving.

She came right up, put her arms around me, and gave me a big hug.

I felt like a traitor. I was here to undermine this woman who obviously took her religion very seriously, even if I didn't understand exactly what it was.

She didn't give Darren the same kind of response. She just said, "Hello," sort of coolly. I guess she knew why we were there.

I felt like crying even more than before. I didn't know what to say. Finally, I blurted out, "Your house looks so nice, I wish I was Jewish."

I don't know why I said that. I felt like a damn fool.

Esther's mother started to laugh. "Well, I think Esther would change places with you. She's not so happy about it."

"Mom," Esther pleaded.

I could see Esther was mortified.

"One thing though," I said — I figured as long as I'd already made a fool out of myself, I might as well go for it. "One thing — I'd be so upset if I'd worked and worked since summer and couldn't compete with the team."

"Well, that's exactly what Esther said, but if we make an exception for this, we'll have to make exceptions about other things like eating pork or eating milk and meat together."

"Is that what being Jewish is?" I asked. "Eating certain things and not eating certain things and not competing on Saturday? No exceptions?"

"No — of course not," Esther said seriously, and she started telling me a whole bunch of stuff about what it was to be Jewish and what they believed, which didn't sound all that different from being Christian. "Do not do unto others what you would not have them do unto you," she said. That sounded familiar. Christians say the same thing in a different way. "Do unto others as you would have them do unto you."

Esther's mother seemed pretty pleased with all the stuff Esther was saying, and it was interesting. I sort of forgot why we were there until her mother said, "That touched me, darling girl, and so did Kisha's question, which you answered so beautifully. There are many rules for religious people to follow. Most of us don't follow all of them. We choose those we can and make them our rules, but it seems to me, it's just as sinful to be inflexible, especially when it will hurt people."

"Does that mean — ," I asked, jumping up and down.

Esther's mother smiled. "As long as she doesn't eat any pork chops."

Esther and I hugged each other.

"Next Friday night, we'll set a place for you," her mother said. "We don't look for converts to our religion, but we'd love to have you partake with us."

■ ■ ■

"Well, you saved the day," Darren said when we got back into the car.

"Yeah, I did, didn't I? Of course, Esther didn't do so bad herself."

16

Darren tried to get us to nap on the road to Los Angeles. Right. As if we could even close our eyes. I couldn't speak for the other kids, but this was the first time I'd ever been outside the Bay Area, and I wasn't about to miss one minute of this trip.

The van barely made it up some of the hills, but that was okay. We'd have gotten out and walked to L.A.

Darren kept saying, "If you don't rest your mouths now, you're gonna be too tired to run when you get there."

But we just kept laughing and talking and singing, and fixing each other's hair, although no one could do anything with mine.

The time passed so quickly we were there before we got a chance to sing half the songs we knew.

We rolled into the parking lot of the West Los

Angeles College Stadium. There were hundreds of cars in the lot already. And kids were piling out of them.

I could have died I was so excited and proud to be there. Of course, I acted real cool, just like the other girls from Whitman. This was the big time. This was for real. This was serious.

I looked at the girls on the other teams. They were all dressed up in these slick, spandex outfits. You could hardly call them uniforms, even though they were, because they were so beautiful. Like something you'd see in a Miss America pageant. And every color you could think of. All perfect and spotless.

Our team sat in the van, just staring at them as they got out of their fancy new cars. They were lucky. Their parents were there with them. They unloaded Thermos jugs and picnic baskets, like the ones you see in the movies, and set up picnics out of the trunks of their cars, with real dishes and silverware. It was amazing.

"Come on," Darren shouted. "Out! Out! Move around. Flex those muscles, get those legs moving."

We all piled out, and Darren went around to the back door of the van, opened it, and set up *our* picnic.

I can't say that I wouldn't have preferred eating what the kids parked next to us were eating. They had sliced chicken sandwiches and fruit salad, with all kinds of fruit, not just what was overripe and cheap. But I wouldn't have traded my team for any other team in the country. We were there for ourselves and for each other. All of us. And what the hell, eating peanut butter sandwiches out of brown paper bags wasn't that bad. Darren called it high energy food, and that's all we needed — high energy.

We ate fast and started cleaning up, just like the other teams. Esther and I walked over to the big garbage can so we could dump the remains. Not that there was so much left except for a few scraps.

Two of the girls from another team were just walking away. I opened my mouth to say "hi" to them, but I couldn't catch their eye.

"They're from the ghetto," one of the girls whispered loudly to the other.

"I know. They're low income. Can you believe those tacky uniforms."

They giggled and walked back to their team, whispering things I wished I hadn't heard.

Esther and I couldn't even look at each other. I wanted to disappear. Our uniforms *were* tacky. They were ugly. Ugly. Ugly. Khaki. Wrinkled from the long trip.

I felt sick.

We walked back slowly. The other kids were very quiet. Nobody was talking or singing anymore.

"Come on," Darren said, clapping his hands, barely able to hold back his enthusiasm. Obviously, he hadn't heard any of the remarks. "Time to get up to the stadium."

We followed him without saying a word.

Esther dropped the baton on the second lap around the track. She reached down to pick it up, but we lost so much time we might as well have given up right there and then. But we were too embarrassed to walk off the track, so we kept up the pretense.

I tripped during the 200-meter race and fell flat on my face, which was bad enough, but it threw the twins off balance, and they ran last and next to last — except for me. I was dead last.

Natonia didn't even place in the Triple Jump, and she was better than anyone else on our team. She'd jumped farther at home than any of the girls who placed.

Alisha twisted her ankle during the Long Jump and limped off the track.

We didn't take one medal. After all our work.

We straggled back to the car after the awards were handed out. Darren had said we had to stay to watch, but we didn't really want to.

The kids in the car next to ours had won three medals. They were singing and laughing and carrying on until they saw us, then they just stopped and stared at us until we got into the van.

As we crawled into our seats, I wished we had one of those fancy cars with tinted windows so I could shut out the rest of the world.

"I'm proud of you," Darren said, as he pulled out of the parking lot.

We asked him was he crazy? Proud of what? We were losers.

"You're winners in my book," he said.

He tooted the horn, just like we'd taken every medal.

"I'm gonna take you out for pizza to celebrate," he said.

None of us was hungry.

"You'll be hungry by the time we get there."

We drove for a while. I wasn't paying too much attention to where we were, then Darren pulled into a Shakey's Pizza restaurant. None of us had any money, but he said it was his treat. Like we had something to celebrate.

He asked us what we wanted.

"Whatever," we said.

So he ordered.

He was more or less keeping up a one-sided conversation.

When the pizzas came, he dug in, but most of us just picked at our food.

"I know how you feel," he said finally.

"How would you know?" Natonia snapped.

"I know," he repeated.

"Look at you," Alisha said. "You dress nice. You live in a nice place, drive a nice car, have a family — "

"Right, Darren," one of the twins said. "You're not a loser. Doubt if you ever have been."

"Don't pick on him," the other twin said.

It was the first time I'd ever heard them disagree.

"I agree with you, Twin," I said, but I knew what the other kids were saying, too. Darren *was* different from us. We had known that right away. We just forgot it for a while.

"Don't call me Twin," she said. "My name's Malika and hers is Shanika."

"Anybody failing in school?" Darren asked.

"No," we all answered.

"Anybody pregnant?" he asked.

We all giggled, despite our mood. "No."

"Anybody taking drugs?" he asked.

"No!" we all shouted.

"See, I told you, you were winners," he said.

Well, he didn't actually convince us, but we were starting to feel a little better. I picked up a piece of pizza. It wasn't bad.

"I was a *real* loser once," Darren said softly. "I didn't just lose a medal in a race."

147

We looked at him, not sure where he was going. He got that faraway look in his eyes, like he did sometimes.

"Remember when I told you I had to learn some things the hard way?" he asked.

We all nodded our heads.

"This is pretty difficult for me to talk about even now. But the summer I graduated from high school, I thought I was the biggest winner of all. I'd been accepted to Berkeley. The first one in my family to go to college. My parents had worked hard for that. They'd come west and started with nothing. At that time, my father was the janitor in the school you all go to and my mother cleaned houses. But by the time I finished high school, my father owned his own business, and my mother was vice president of a bank. They owned the kind of house my mother used to clean. They were proud of me. Me? I just took everything I had for granted.

"At a party one night I got drunk — very drunk. Despite everything my parents had ever told me about drinking. Despite the problems other kids I knew got into because of it. Anyway, I wound up embarrassing myself, my family, my friends. Instead of going to Berkeley, I spent eleven months in jail for aiding and abetting a criminal act."

We were shocked. What could we say? Darren

in *jail,* like some drug pusher or junkie? Why was he telling us this? It wasn't something I really wanted to know.

"When I got out, I couldn't get a job. I'd learned computers in jail, but no one would hire me."

"So you came to Whitman," Natonia said. "They'd hire anybody. I swear if I die and go to hell, I'll recognize it 'cause I'm sure it'll look just like Whitman."

"Eventually, I found my way to Whitman. But I spent a few years feeling sorry for myself first," Darren said. "I hid out, couldn't face anyone, except Lureen, who stood by me even after I messed up so bad. I felt like the biggest loser of all time. And then I got Lureen pregnant, and I *knew* I couldn't do anything right. I was an even bigger loser. By the time I'd applied for the job at Whitman, I was twenty-four years old, and I'd just about given up on myself."

We all moved in closer to Darren, shouting that he was the best coach there ever was. "We love you. You're a winner."

"Yeah," Darren said. "I am now."

By the time we got back to Oakland, we were ready to collapse. It had been a confusing day. No matter what Darren said, we still felt like losers. And I could still hear the whispers of the girls from the other teams. I was sure everyone else could, too, but none of us said a word about it.

As he dropped each of us off, as he always did after dark, we quietly said good-bye and disappeared.

I knew Tyrone and my mom would be waiting up for me, even though it was after two o'clock in the morning. And I felt almost worse for them than for me.

I unlocked the door and walked in. "Hi," I whispered softly.

No one answered. I had this fleeting moment of panic, the way you do sometimes when you feel in your bones something's wrong, but you don't know what it is. I could feel the hair stand up on my arms, and my heart started to beat faster.

"Mom," I whispered.

"Kisha?" she whispered back.

She was in the living room, but the lights were off.

"I must have fallen asleep," she said.

I walked over to turn on the light.

"Don't," she said. "My eyes can't take it."

"I'll turn it on low."

"Just leave it off," she said. "There's enough light from outside. Come sit next to me and tell me about the meet."

She sat up on the couch to make room for me. I

hesitated for a minute, caught between the need to fall in her lap and cry on the one hand, and the need to act grown up on the other.

I was so tired that everything seemed eerie and unreal, especially in the dark. It was almost as if the whole day was my worst nightmare, and I was still dreaming it. One minute I was reliving the humiliation of falling on my face in front of hundreds of people, and the next I was floating above it all, detached, as if it had happened to someone else who was related to me, but not really me. I couldn't shake the feeling I'd had when I first came in — something was wrong.

I waited for my mother to give me some hint of what it might be.

"Did you bring back any medals?" she asked.

"No. I messed up. We all did."

"Next time," she said.

I wanted to tell her there wasn't going to be a next time. I had made a fool out of myself once. I wasn't going to try it a second time. My dad had been right all along. I had no business on the track team.

"I'm tired," I said.

"I bet. Why don't you sack out? We can talk about it tomorrow."

She was saying all the right words, but the music was wrong. Flat. As if she wasn't herself, either.

"What?" I asked.

"I said, we can talk tomorrow."

Some inner voice kept whispering to me, but the words were all mixed up. All I knew was that I had this urge to turn on the light. I had to.

I walked over to the table and reached up.

"Please, don't," my mother said.

"Why?" I asked, but I didn't wait for an answer. I turned the little black knob once, and the table came into focus. I turned it again. The couch was entirely visible. My mother got up and gathered up the blanket she had thrown over her. Her back was to me as if she were trying to shut me out of her life. As I suspected, my coming home without a medal had hurt her more than me.

It made me mad. I needed her support now, not her criticism, and I felt her silence was just that. Criticism.

Angrily, I turned up the light another notch. The whole room lit up. Still, she kept her back to me.

"I'm going to bed," I said.

I wanted her to turn around and hug me, tell me she thought I was wonderful, even though I knew I wasn't.

She didn't. And I didn't approach her.

I just reached up and turned the light off.

17

I slept till noon on Sunday and awoke to the same eerie silence I had felt when I walked in the night before. Before I even opened my eyes, I could feel aches creeping up and down my body. Even my mind and soul ached.

I burrowed farther under the covers and pulled them over my head.

"You up?" Ty whispered.

"No," I mumbled.

He didn't say anything else, but I could feel his eyes boring right through the covers. I slid them down as slowly as I could.

"Okay, I'm up."

"Shush."

"It's after twelve. No one else is sleeping, are they?"

"I have to talk to you," he said urgently.

I sat up. The panic started creeping up on me again.

"Did you see her last night?"

"Who?"

"She made me go to bed. I tried to wait up for you, but I couldn't."

"What?"

"Didn't you see her?"

"I saw her."

He searched my face.

"I saw her," I repeated.

"She said she bumped into the kitchen door."

"What's that supposed to mean?" I asked. I could hear my voice getting higher.

"Her eye. Didn't you notice?"

"It was dark."

"I was at choir practice at the center. When I came back she was in the kitchen cooking. I didn't think anything, then she turned around, and I saw she had this shiner. We just stood there looking at each other. Then she said that about the kitchen door. I didn't believe her. She knew I didn't. That's why she wouldn't let me stay up with her."

"Where is he?"

"He was gone when I got home. I don't know if he came back, or not."

"Did you see him this morning?"

"I've been waiting for you to get up."

"I'm going to the bathroom," I said.

I needed time to think.

I brushed my teeth and washed my face, then I washed and brushed again. It probably did my teeth some good, but it didn't help my brain any. Thoughts were going around in it, but none of them made any sense.

All this stuff was happening, and I couldn't take it in. My brain felt like a pot that was so full it kept overflowing. Only someone kept pouring in more water anyway. And I was swimming around under it all. It was like I was hearing and seeing everything, but I was underwater so nothing was clear.

When I came back to the room, Ty was still sitting there, waiting for me to come up with something. And I still didn't know what to do.

"It's like World War III," he said.

"Yeah," I said.

"Even if the war hits your neighborhood, you never think it's gonna hit your house."

"I know," I said, feeling totally stupid. What was I supposed to do? I was the oldest. Ty was counting on me.

"What should we do?"

"Go out there, I guess."

Ty hung in back of me, and we walked into the kitchen. Mom was sitting reading the newspaper. Her face was half-hidden, but I could see she had a black eye that was turning six different colors at the same time.

I could have cried right then and there, but I didn't. I don't know why exactly, but I didn't.

"How 'bout I make us some breakfast?" I said, being real cheery, like Mom is sometimes when things are the worst.

"Thanks, honey," she said.

"I'll help," Ty offered.

The two of us got busy, making pancake batter and heating up the syrup. I glanced over at the counter. No coffee cup. I put up a pot of coffee. It made me feel better being busy. I cracked three eggs in a bowl and beat them up for scrambled eggs.

Ty set the plates on the counter, and I set out the food. Mom smiled at us. We smiled back nervously. Then we all ate breakfast.

And I knew we'd done the right thing. If she wanted to tell us what happened to her eye, she would. If not, we would all just pretend what she wanted us to — that she walked into the kitchen door.

Ty and I hung out at the house for the rest of the afternoon, just playing around, keeping our eyes on

Mom. She was quiet, more quiet than usual, but all the tension and panic I'd felt last night and this morning seemed to be melting away. Maybe I'd just gotten used to it, and it felt normal. Maybe you get used to anything after you get over the first shock.

Around dinner time, Natonia came knocking at the door. At first she didn't want to come in, but I kind of told her, without coming right out and telling her, that my dad wasn't home. So she came in, and we went into my room. Ty and Mom were playing cards in the living room.

We talked around what happened at the meet, but neither of us really talked *about* it. I didn't know why Natonia came over, but I was happy she was there. It was almost like old times.

"I been thinking about moving on," Natonia said as she rolled over on the bed.

"Moving on?" I asked. "You mean going back to Darren's?"

"No. I mean leaving Darren's altogether."

"How come? Anybody else would change places with you in a minute."

"I heard them talking last night. Him and Lureen. She said the apartment was too small for me to be staying there."

"Shoot."

"And that's true, I guess. One bedroom, and all."

"Shoot."

"I don't know. I been thinking. Maybe I'll try to find my mom in San Francisco."

"You know where she lives?"

"Well, not exactly."

"You just going to go looking for her?"

"Why not?"

"Maybe your grandmother knows where she is. Let's go find out. Come on. I'll go with you."

"I don't want to go over there."

"She loves you, Natonia. I know she does."

"I know she does, too," Natonia said. "So do my uncles. Too much. That's the problem."

At first I just stared at her. I thought I knew what she meant. But at the same time, I couldn't be right. Could I? Her own uncles!

"That sucks," I said finally. "That really sucks."

"Yeah."

"Does she know? Your grandmother."

"She knows, and she doesn't know."

"I think we ought to tell her. I think she'll throw those lazy dogs out of the house."

"No, she won't," Natonia said.

"She'll have to."

"She won't."

"How can you be so sure?"

"Like she says, she can't control her boys. Never could. But they pay the rent. That's just the reality of it."

"Reality sucks," I said, and Natonia agreed.

Of course, that didn't exactly solve her problem or mine either, for that matter.

I wanted to ask Natonia to spend the night with us, but I was too scared. What if my dad came home? Then we'd both be even worse off than we were now.

"Darren know where you are?" I asked.

"No. They went out. I just left. Walked over here."

"All that way?"

"Yeah."

"Well, you can't walk back. It's getting dark."

"Who cares?" Natonia said.

"Me. I do," I said. I just couldn't believe it. Every *day*, my life got more and more complicated.

We just sat there, staring into space. We heard the phone ring. Heard my mom get up and go into the kitchen to answer it. Heard her say, "Hello. Yes. She is. No, that's all right. Yes, I agree with you. It's up to her. Okay," she said, then she hung up, and we could hear her walking back toward my bedroom.

She knocked on the door. She didn't barge in like some other mothers did.

"That was Darren," she said. "He was worried about you, Natonia. Said he figured you might be here."

"Uh huh," Natonia said, like she didn't care, but I saw her neck muscles tighten up, and I knew she did.

"Natonia, if it's all right with you, he wants to come get you. He doesn't want you walking back in the dark."

"No," she said. "He don't really want to come get me."

"Well, that's what he said on the phone."

"Maybe he does, but Lureen doesn't."

"I see," my mom said, and she came over and gave Natonia a hug. "Why don't we invite Darren to come over, so we can all talk about this. Maybe we can figure something out together. I'm not sure, but I had the feeling he might have an idea about what to do."

"He always does," Natonia said, sarcastically, sounding more like her old self.

"Does that mean it's okay if I tell him to come?"

"Your house."

"You're our guest."

"It's all right," Natonia said.

Well, Darren came over, and as usual, he had something up his sleeve. "You know we love having you stay with us," he said to Natonia.

We both tensed up. We knew what was going to come after that announcement. Nothing but bad news. But we were wrong. More or less.

"You know I've been hanging around the school all year," Darren went on, "and — "

"I been doing my work," Natonia said. "Most of the time."

"I know," Darren said. "I was just going to say that I'm pretty friendly with some of the teachers."

We stuck our fingers in our mouths and pretended to gag.

"A few of them."

We put our fingers around our necks as if we were choking.

"One of them."

"Ms. Collins," Natonia and I said together.

"Yeah. Layla Collins. She was a couple of years ahead of me in school. And she was a lot smarter. Smarter than most of the teachers."

"She's cool," I said.

"What's that got to do with me?" Natonia asked, her head cocked to one side as if she just couldn't trust what Darren was going to say.

"She likes you a lot, Natonia," he said.

"So?" Natonia said.

"She'd like you to come stay with her."

"I don't like all this moving around. I've been thinking of going to look for my mom," Natonia said.

I could see she was trying to keep her pride, that the thought of being shifted around from house to house like some foster child didn't particularly appeal to her.

"I can understand that," Darren said, "but I have an idea. Why don't you stay at Ms. Collins's place until we can locate your mother?"

"Maybe."

"I'll see what I can do," Darren promised. "I have some friends on the San Francisco police force."

"Does she really want me, or does she think she'd be doing me this big favor? 'Cause I don't want no favors from nobody."

"I think she wants you," Darren said, "but it won't be a free ride, by any means. She'll expect you to help with dinner, with cleaning the house, stuff like that. Be a real part of her family."

"How many people in her family?"

"Just her, and she has two bedrooms. You'd have your own room."

"Maybe," Natonia said.

"Do it," I urged.

"My own room?"

"Yeah."

"I guess I could talk to her."

"She's in the car," Darren said.

18

Turns out Ms. Collins is okay out of school, too. She doesn't hassle Natonia any, doesn't ask questions. It's almost like she's a real mother to her, only better. Just about every day, there she is, standing beside the track when we run. Even when it's cold. She pulls up the collar on her coat, bundles her arms around herself, stamps her feet to keep warm, and cheers us on when we come around to where she's standing. It almost makes it seem worthwhile. It's like we almost want to go on. But we don't really. The enthusiasm just drained out of us after the meet in Los Angeles. Like this tiny hole was bored into us, and the enthusiasm seeped out, little by little, until there wasn't any left.

We came to work out and run, I guess because of Darren. It sure wasn't because we felt that we were still in training. But it had gotten to be a habit, and sometimes you just do things because you've always done them. Seems like I couldn't remember not going to the community center after school.

Jennifer's dad and Darren kept us at it. Like the L.A. meet hadn't even happened. Like we could still be winners, if we wanted to. Well, dream on. The team was a little more realistic than our coaches, but, in a sense, we couldn't let them down.

I don't know. Maybe that's the thing with adults. They're always talking about us playing our games, but they're the ones who play the games. They're always play-acting with each other, and pretending it's real life. Even Ms. Collins. She's playing at being Natonia's mother. Which isn't bad. Don't get me wrong. Natonia should only be so lucky. But still, it's a game. Natonia's been around. She knows it can't last forever.

Then there's my mother and father. The biggest actors of all time. Funny, how one day you don't understand anything, and the next you wonder how things have been going on under your nose for years, and you were blind to them.

They never said a word about the black eye. Not a word. Never said where he was for two days, either. And point is, last year, I probably wouldn't have even noticed. He'd disappeared before, and my mom would just say, "Dad's gone over to San Francisco to see a friend." As if that was an excuse. San Francisco was only a half-hour away! He was just too drunk to get home.

But now I pick up these little clues. I see that she's stopped talking about what she does at school. At least in front of him. And I see that he doesn't pay so much attention to the way he dresses, like he used to. Everyone used to say my dad was the handsomest guy in our project. I don't know anymore. Something's different. Even in the way he walks. But they just go on pretending things are just like they've always been. We eat our meals together like a TV family, but the food doesn't taste the same.

Nothing about my life is the same — except running track. I ran it yesterday. I'll run it today. And I'll probably be out there running it tomorrow.

When we got to the center after school, nobody felt like going out to the track. Nobody felt like doing anything except lying around at the center, listening to music.

When Darren came out from his office, that's exactly what we were doing. We hadn't even changed into our workout clothes.

"Hey," he yelled. "Get your butts in gear!"

We all moaned. This play-acting had gone on long enough.

Only Darren still had any illusions left about our being track stars.

We reluctantly climbed up the stairs to change, then we trekked back down again and went through the paces, but none of us could really get into it.

"Come on, grab your coats," Darren yelled. "I have a surprise."

The surprise was the old van. His friend had donated it to our team so we would have transportation from the center to the track without squeezing into Darren's car.

A month ago, we would have gone crazy at the thought of having our own car, but now we all looked at it and remembered the shiny new cars in the parking lot of the West Los Angeles College Stadium. We piled in without saying a word.

Darren was taking a new route I noticed, as I glumly looked out of the window. No one even felt like talking anymore.

About halfway to nowhere, the van started sputtering, then it wound down like a toy whose battery had run out.

Darren pushed on the gas pedal. The van jerked and lurched forward, then came to a dead stop.

"I knew it," Alisha said, "What could you expect out of this ancient piece of garbage?"

"Sitting on top of each other in your car was better than this," Natonia said.

"What are we supposed to do? Get out and push?" Esther asked.

"Exactly," Darren said, opening the car door and getting out.

"Are you crazy?" I yelled.

Even Shanika and Malika were rolling their eyes, as if Darren had finally flipped out.

"No gas," Darren said. "You're gonna have to push it to the gas station."

"We!" we all cried.

"You. I gotta steer," Darren said. "I'm the only one with a driver's license."

He showed us how to push and where, then he got back in the car and released the brake.

We grumbled all the way, huffing and puffing, swearing that we weren't going another step, yelling at Darren to pull over to the side, so we could abandon the old piece of tin. But we pushed the van up one hill after another until we came to a gas station. We were so mad we wouldn't even look at Darren when he got out of the car. It was his stupidity that got us into this mess in the first place.

He filled the tank. We got back into the van and collapsed.

"It's December. It's going to be dark pretty soon! I

hope you don't expect us to run track today," Malika said angrily.

"Of course not," Darren answered. "This was the best exercise you've had in weeks."

It was the way he said it, with a sort of smile in his voice, that clued us in. At first we couldn't believe it, then Shanika asked, "Did you do that on purpose?"

"Had to find some way to get you guys going."

We screamed and beat on his head, but the whole incident did kind of get rid of a lot of frustration. It's hard to say why, but it did. Afterward, we all laughed.

When we got back to the center we were all going to leave for home, but Darren started talking about getting ready for The Athletic Congress Nationals. Just as casual as could be. As if that's what we'd been planning on doing all along. The Nationals. Us. We'd only been to one other meet — which was disastrous, to say the least. We all laughed — uncomfortably at first, then downright nervously. If he was serious about this somebody was gonna be very disappointed.

"One of the problems with Los Angeles was that you were all so tired by the time we got there," Darren explained. "It was too much, getting up in the middle of the night and driving all the way to L.A., and then running the same afternoon. The other kids had an advantage over us to start with. They either spent the night in Los Angeles, or came from around the area. We're not going to make that mistake again."

He laughed. "We can't. The TAC is in Hershey, Pennsylvania."

"You mean we can't drive there in one day?" Alisha asked.

"We're gonna have to fly," Darren said.

It was our turn to laugh. None of us had ever been on an airplane. When you wonder how many nights in a row you can take beans for dinner, you don't think about flying around the country. Trust Darren to forget that plane tickets cost money. Maybe he could fly wherever he wanted to. But we couldn't.

"Look, I know plane tickets cost money," he said as if he could read my mind.

"No kidding," Alisha said.

"We've got three months," Darren said. "I've been saving the money from our bake sales. I've been going around to businesses for donations. We have enough for track shoes. We have enough for most of the tickets."

"You got money for shoes? For all of us?" Esther asked.

"Think I've been loafing on the job?" Darren asked.

"When're we going to get them?" Natonia demanded, as if she didn't really believe Darren.

"Tomorrow after practice. Now listen up. We're not

there yet. We still have to raise more money. So I want you all to go home and start baking. We're gonna have bake sales at the center twice a week from now till March."

"I ain't going," Alisha said sullenly.

We all looked at her.

"I ain't going out there to make a fool out of myself in those tacky rejects from the Army/Navy store."

"Me neither, Darren," Natonia said.

We all agreed.

"When you go shopping for the shoes tomorrow, maybe we can run over to the fabric store and pick out material," Ms. Collins said.

Nobody had seen her come in, but she was standing by the door, and she'd obviously been listening to our conversation.

"We can't sew," Shanika said.

"I can," Ms. Collins said. "And I have a sewing machine."

"My mom can," I said. "Maybe she could help."

We started getting caught up in the excitement of it all. Getting track shoes, making hot pink spandex outfits that glittered in the sunlight and about knocked your eyes out. Ms. Collins showed us how to cut out the patterns and baste them, then she and my mom sewed them up on her machine. When we finally all tried them on at the same time, we couldn't believe how we looked. We congratulated each other. We were all beautiful. And no one could tell our outfits were home-made.

We ran around the room, our arms flapping like the wings of the airplane we would soon be boarding. None of us considered exactly why we were doing all this. None of us remembered that we had silently agreed not to run in a track meet again — ever. The plans just started taking hold and snowballing so fast that we got caught up in them.

And practice seemed to be going better. Somehow we were running faster and jumping higher than ever.

Some days a few of the mothers would show up at the track and cheer us on. My mother. Shanika and Malika's mother and sometimes their father. Jennifer's father, of course. And Ms. Collins. We never felt like we were competing against each other. It was more like we were proud of each other. We were showing off our friends for our mothers. We all wanted to do well, so they'd be proud of us.

Of course, I wouldn't be totally honest if I didn't admit that I also liked winning, and the twins were clearly competing against each other, too. They even started dressing differently. Hell, they looked different. For the first time I noticed that Shanika was about an inch shorter then Malika, and the shape of their eyes was different.

One day, even Lureen showed up at the track. Of course, I was prepared to continue disliking her, especially given what she'd said about Natonia, and all. But she was so friendly and encouraging, it was hard not to respond. And she'd also brought along a big Thermos of hot chocolate for us, so it was hard to stay mad at her.

We didn't think Darren was going to let us drink the hot chocolate, but he did. Maybe because Lureen had brought it, and he was just pleased about that.

But food was a big issue with all of us. And this time, when we went to the meet in Hershey, Pennsylvania, we wouldn't be eating peanut butter sandwiches while the other kids had their fancy picnics. This time Darren said we could eat in real restaurants.

Even the name — Hershey, Pennsylvania — sounded special to me. Like a kiss.

19

"If I have to make one more cookie," I screamed, "I'm gonna die!"

We had two weeks to go, and we still didn't have enough money to get all of us to Hershey, Pennsylvania. For one thing, as one of our mothers pointed out, and I'm sure it was mine, there should be a female adult along on the trip since we were staying overnight in a motel. Now, that just goes to show you where a mother's head is. As if we would have anything else on our minds but the meet. Besides Darren would kill us dead on the spot if he found us fooling around. But whoever it was — my mother, or someone else's — Darren agreed. Of course, he wouldn't have thought of it, if it hadn't been drawn to his attention. Which shows you where his mind is: On the track, where it should be.

"How much more do you need?" my mother whispered to me as I stood in the kitchen, wondering if I could get that hand mixer to work one more time.

"Two hundred dollars," I said, absent-mindedly. "Why are you whispering?"

"Are there any more businesses that might contribute?"

"Sure," I said, sarcastically. "Maybe Natonia can go down to Mr. Abrakus's market and ask him. We've asked everyone else in town. The supermarket gave us a hundred. He didn't say so, but I think Darren's put in some of his own money, and his parents donated two hundred. Ms. Collins paid for all the material for our outfits. The twins' parents gave what they could. And Jennifer's dad made a big contribution, but nobody's supposed to know about it. I just happened to overhear him and Darren talking about it. I'm not sure how much, but I think it was a lot. Darren said, 'I can't take this, Pat. Teachers aren't exactly raking it in.'"

"You can say that again," my mother said.

She was talking to me, but she wasn't. I could tell her mind was on something else. Like it was lots of times lately.

A few months ago, I could barely get her off my back. She always had to know where I was going. How long was I going to be there? Who else was going to be there. I had to call her before I walked home. I couldn't be anyplace after dark without her. Now it seems like she doesn't even know I'm around half the time. It's like she's said to herself, *Well, Kisha's all grown up now. She can make her own decisions.*

But as long as I keep my mind on track, things seem pretty clear-cut. There are rules. You know what they are. They don't change on you out of the blue. You know who you can count on to run the 400 meter. Who you can count on to jump. At least as long as we're training. The weird thing is, the way the slightest thing can shift the balance. We're in a different place, and suddenly it's as if we're different people.

Maybe what we have to do is concentrate more. Say to ourselves — *this is who I am. I'm the most valuable relay runner.* Period. Don't think about what you can't do as well. Think about what you *can* do. And do it.

That all seems pretty clear to me while I'm standing in my kitchen, but I'm not sure how I'm going to feel when I get to Hershey, Pennsylvania. There's this little part of me that hopes we don't actually come up with all the money we need. Because as excited as I am about going, about taking an airplane to get there, I'm not sure how I'm going to feel with all those hundreds of people watching me. I still trip over my own feet sometimes.

"I guess I'll make brownies again," I muttered to

175

myself as I took the flour out of the cupboard. What a way to spend a Sunday afternoon.

"Where's Ty?" my mother asked.

"At choir practice."

"I'm glad he's interested in something besides war. That's all you see on TV these days. It's enough to depress you in a big way."

"Ty says the whole world's gonna blow up."

"Well, I can't see that happening, but who knows? The Bible says first there'll be flood, then fire will scorch the earth and go down to the sea, and — "

"What!"

"Of course, it doesn't say how long between the fire and the total end of the world."

"When you look at it that way, makes everything else seem pretty dumb. I mean, if the world's gonna end, why am I worried about baking these brownies?"

"Because it most probably *isn't* going to end tomorrow. You can't stop living just because something *might* happen. Best thing you can do is go on with your life and make the best of it. If enough people do that, maybe someone might come up with a solution one of these days."

"Maybe Ty."

"I don't know. I can't always follow what's going on with these countries at war. It seems to be like a kid's game. You do that to me. I'll do worse to you. I can't understand why they can't just sit down and talk about it instead of trying to blow each other up."

"I guess for the same reason ordinary people don't," I said, thinking about how Alisha and Natonia would sometimes get so mad at each other that they'd start yelling and screaming about anything and everything except what they were really mad about. And occasionally they'd take a swing at each other.

Even when I got mad at Natonia we still didn't sit down and talk about it. I just carried it around with me for a while till I could push it down far enough to forget about it. What I wondered though was where it went when I pushed it down.

"I'm going to run out for a few minutes," my mother said as she picked up her pocketbook.

"Sure," I said. "You just don't want to get roped into helping me out with the brownies."

"That's right," she said.

Just as I was shoving the brownies into the oven, my father walked into the kitchen. We grunted at each other. It wasn't that we were mad at each other, or anything like that, it was just that things had sort of changed. Not so you could notice things had changed unless you knew us last year and hadn't had any contact with us for a year. It had happened gradually. It wasn't one day we were a family and the next day we weren't. It was that, little by little, the family sort of got eaten away, and now, for the most part we were just people living in the same house.

There were times when me and my mom were part of a family. Or me and Ty were brother and sister, but generally speaking, there weren't many times when the four of us were all together. Since my mom was working and my dad wasn't, they sort of kept different hours. And I was always training or doing my homework, and Ty was running off to choir practice or lying in front of the TV watching the news. It was as if we didn't have all that much to say to each other anymore.

"What you got for breakfast?" my father asked.

"It's two o'clock in the afternoon," I said.

"I'm not asking you what time it is. I'm asking what we have to eat in this here house."

"Eggs," I said, without looking at him.

"I don't feel like eggs."

"We had eggs."

"I don't care what you had. Never anything you want in this house when you want it."

I could have offered to make him some grits or pancakes, or something like that. I had noticed a few slices of bacon in the refrigerator, but I figured he wasn't crippled, he could open it up, see what he wanted, and make it himself.

"Where's everybody at?" he asked as he slipped into a seat at the kitchen counter.

"I'm here," I offered. "Don't know where anybody else is."

"Got any aspirin?"

"I don't know. Maybe in the bathroom."

"I got a bad headache."

He's giving me one, too, I thought. Five minutes to go on the brownies. If I hadn't been waiting for them, I'd have been out of there already.

"Maybe if you took a shower, you'd feel better," I said.

"Don't you go telling me what to do," he said, sneering at me.

He didn't have to jump down my throat. I was just trying to be helpful. Even if *he* didn't feel better if he took a shower, I would. He looked like he hadn't taken one in days. Smelled like it, too. And he obviously hadn't bothered to brush his teeth this morning, either.

"Everybody around here telling me what to do all of a sudden," he mumbled. "Like a man doesn't have a mind of his own anymore."

Yeah, yeah, yeah, I wanted to say. But I didn't.

179

"Where'd she go?"

"I told you. I don't know."

"When she leave?"

"Not too long ago."

"She go to the store?"

"Don't know."

"She must have gone to the store."

"Maybe."

"She take her pocketbook?"

"I don't know. Yeah, she did. I remember she picked it up from the counter."

"That's what I thought. What's to eat?"

"Why don't you wait till she comes back from the store?"

"Haven't eaten anything since yesterday morning."

I figured he was trying to make me feel sorry for him, but I wasn't going to buy into that one again.

The timer went off for the brownies, and I jumped.

I took them out of the oven and put them on the counter to cool off.

"I'll have one of them," he said.

"They're for the bake sale."

"They're always for the bake sale. Think we're made of money, or something? Think you can just bake anything you want, anytime you want?"

"No."

"Then give me one."

"They're still hot."

"I don't care."

"Take it yourself," I said. "I've got to go."

I slammed out of the house, leaving him at the kitchen counter. He could eat the whole pan of brownies as far as I was concerned.

I started walking, but I didn't know where I was walking *to*. Anyplace away from him was good enough, I figured.

I was headed in the direction of Malika and Shanika's house, so I just kept on walking that way.

When I got there, I knocked on the door. I waited, but no one answered. I sat down on their stoop for a while, but they must have gone someplace for the afternoon with their family, the way we used to do.

I checked my watch. Three-thirty. Ty would be finishing up with choir practice. I decided to go over there and walk home with him.

He was coming out of the building when I rounded the corner.

"How come Mom was here?" he asked.

"Mom?"

"Yeah. She was here a little while ago."

"I don't know. She talk to Darren?"

"Not that I know of. I just saw her come in and out."

"Weird."

"I thought maybe you knew."

"No."

"How come you're here?"

"I don't know. Nothing else to do."

"Mom tell you to walk me home?"

"Would she tell me to do that?"

"Yeah."

"Would I do it if she told me to?"

"No."

"That answer your question?"

God, was everybody freaking out, or what? We walked the rest of the way home in silence, both of us kicking stones along the way.

When we got to the front door, we heard screaming and yelling coming from our apartment. We stopped and stood there. For a minute I thought maybe I should take Ty and leave, but somehow I couldn't.

"Ever since you got that job, you've been thinking you can run things around here," my father yelled. "I knew it! I knew this would happen!"

"Somebody has to run things around here," my mother said.

"I worked all my life," he said. "Is it my fault I was laid off?"

"That was two years ago."

"I stuck around because of you and the kids."

"Well, don't let us stop you," she said with this coldness in her voice that made chills run up and down my spine.

There was a long silence, then I heard something crash against the wall.

"It's not here!" he screamed.

"What was that?" I whispered to Ty.

He shrugged his shoulders and grabbed my hand, something he hadn't done in about five years. But I was glad to be holding on to it.

"I know what you're looking for," she said, as if she was putting something over on him. "But you're not going to find it."

"I thought you were at the store."

"I wasn't."

"Didn't you go to the store to cash your check?"

"No."

"It was in here last night."

"You have no business going through my pocket-book."

"What did you do with it?"

"It was my check."

"It was our check. When I had a job, did I say this is my money? No. It was for all of us. Where do you get off saying it was your check?"

"Settle down," she said, like maybe she was sorry she'd gotten him all worked up.

"Where's the check?"

"I can't tell you."

There was another crash, then this long silence. Ty and I held on to each other. Both of us knew the silence wasn't a good one, but we didn't know what was going on.

Then we heard this scream.

"You tell me what you did with it, or I'm gonna whack you."

She mumbled something. We couldn't make out what it was.

"I can't hear you," he said.

"I signed it over to the track team," she cried. "For their trip."

I gasped, but before I had a chance to think about anything, we heard a BANG! Just one. Then another scream and a lot of commotion.

Ty and I were standing there screaming and crying. We didn't know what had happened, but in my mind's eye I could see my mother sprawled out on the kitchen floor, my dad standing over her with a gun.

Then my mind went blank.

20

You hear people say, "Time stood still." You kind of know what it means, but not really. It's one of those expressions that's buried inside of you. But when it happens, when time actually does stand still, you instantly know what it means.

Time was one long scream that ripped through my whole body, a scream that seemed to go on forever. I saw nothing, felt nothing, heard nothing but that scream. The scream propelled me next door to Deandra's house. The scream sent her reeling to the phone.

I think I was still screaming when the police and the ambulance came. I'm not sure if it was real or in my head.

In the distance, someone kept saying that my mother was all right, that it was just her leg, but I couldn't make any sense out of that. Everything had lost its meaning.

Words had become just words, and I couldn't string them together, couldn't understand. I could only feel the scream inside of me.

Men with mustaches whisked past me and ran into the house. They carried a body out on a stretcher. A part of me felt this, though I know I didn't actually see it. A part of me knew the body belonged to my mother, but I couldn't move.

She disappeared into the ambulance.

My father came out of the house and got into the police car. Then one of the policeman came over to where Ty and I were standing. He started talking, but he wasn't making sense. I stared at him blankly. I was glad someone else was answering for me. Or maybe it was me talking, and I didn't recognize my own voice any longer.

I put my hand up to my lips. They were still, but the voice was still coming out. Then slowly I began to defrost. I felt Deandra's arm around me. It was her voice. She was telling the policeman she would take care of things here.

What things? I wondered. *Was I a thing?*

"Are you going to put him in jail?" Ty asked the policeman.

"We're going to take him down to headquarters," the policeman answered.

"Will he be there all night?" Ty asked.

"Yes," the policeman said.

"What about tomorrow?" Ty asked.

"Depends," the policeman said.

"Will he be there for a long time?" Ty asked.

"Probably not."

"Then leave him here and take me," Ty said.

The policeman put his arm around Ty. "What happened isn't your fault, son."

Ty started to cry.

I wanted to tell the policeman that's not what Ty meant. That's not what he meant at all. But I couldn't talk. And maybe it *was* what he meant.

"Come on in the apartment," Deandra said, as she took Ty's hand. She tried to take mine, but I broke loose.

Go into my apartment? Never, I vowed. I closed my eyes and saw blood everywhere.

"Where are you going, Kisha?" Ty asked.

"To Natonia's," I answered.

I don't know how I got there. I'd been there before, when we worked on the uniforms, but I wasn't sure exactly where it was or even what street it was on. I just walked. I don't even remember looking at street signs or stopping to figure out where I was, but somehow I got there.

Only once I was there, I didn't know what to say or

do. I just stood outside the door. I didn't knock. I just stood there shaking.

I guess Ms. Collins opened the door. I guess she must have brought me into the house because I was sitting down in the living room. Natonia was staring at me. I'd seen Natonia in trouble lots of times, but I'd never seen her look so scared. It scared me even more.

I wanted to tell her what had happened. But I didn't know exactly what had happened. I was in a total daze.

Then Darren showed up. I don't know who called him, or how he knew to come, but he was there, telling me that my mother was okay. I heard him, but I didn't believe him. "But I saw the body," I said.

"She was shot in the leg," he said. "I'm going to get her at the hospital and bring her home. Come with me."

"No!"

"I don't like hospitals either," Darren said. "Why don't I pick you up on the way back?"

"I'm not going into that apartment," I said.

"Why don't you stay here with us tonight?" Ms. Collins asked.

"I'm not going back, ever," I said. "I can't."

Ms. Collins and Darren looked at each other.

"I'll go over there with you tomorrow," Natonia said.

"I'm not going," I said.

188

I couldn't understand why they didn't hear me. I knew I should explain, but I couldn't really. What could I tell them? Could I say that my feelings had become numb and the only thing I felt was the scream inside my head? I knew that if I went back into my apartment I would never be able to get away from the sound of that gunshot. It would follow me around for the rest of my life.

Or maybe I should confess. Maybe I should tell them it was my fault because it was really, when you get right down to it.

I knew I was making him mad. I knew it, and I didn't care. What was the big deal? I could have made him breakfast. I could have offered him a brownie. But, no. I just wanted to make him feel bad. And he took it out on her.

I was trouble. People didn't understand that. If they knew, if they understood, they wouldn't want me around.

21

My mother called when she got home from the hospital. There were lots of things I wanted to say to her, but my mind went blank. I was grateful that she was all right. A superficial wound, she said. But deep down I was also mad at her. I don't know why I blamed her for what happened, but in a way I did.

I was polite, and everything. I told her I was glad she was okay, but when she said, "I'll see you tomorrow, then," I didn't answer her. What I wanted to say was, "No, you won't." But I didn't.

Next morning, Ms. Collins woke me up and said it was time for breakfast. I didn't feel much like eating. I got dressed anyway and came into the kitchen. The sun hurt my eyes. The orange juice hurt my stomach. I pushed the bowl of cereal away from me and started to get up. But it felt like someone else was lifting my body from the chair. In fact, it didn't feel like it was my body at all. I pinched myself to make sure my head and my body were still connected. I couldn't feel anything. I pinched harder. I could feel pain, but it didn't seem like it belonged to me.

"Come on, honey, get some food in you before school," Ms. Collins said.

"I can't," I said, weakly. Even the words felt as if they were coming out of somebody else's mouth.

"You gotta," Natonia said. "You saw what happened to me when I didn't eat."

There was a fog in my head. It ached. I got up, walked into the living room and lay down on the couch. I pulled the blanket around me and tried to disappear into the pattern on the couch.

I could feel Natonia and Ms. Collins near me. I wanted to tell them to go on to school without me. But I didn't have the energy to open my mouth.

"We're leaving in a few minutes," Ms. Collins said. "You ready?"

I shook my head, no.

She tried to help me up from the couch. *I can't go outside,* I wanted to tell her.

"I'll stay here with her," Natonia said quietly.

Ms. Collins didn't answer right away, then she let out a sigh. "Okay. I'll get your work at school and bring it home with me."

■ ■ ■

I guess it went on like that for a few days. I lost track of time. Darren came and went. So did the other kids on the team. Even Jennifer.

"Get off the couch, girl, we need you," Alisha said almost angrily. But I knew she wasn't really angry. She was scared.

"You have to start running again, or your muscles will get flabby," Shanika said.

Esther just squeezed my hand, and Jennifer brought me a teddy bear — to borrow, she said. It was a shabby old thing, but maybe it meant something to her.

They came every day after training and tried to joke around as usual. But we all knew something terrible had happened, and we all had to face the fact that Spandex outfits aside, weapons were more of a reality in our lives than trophies or medals.

I appreciated what the team was trying to do for me. I knew they cared about me, but the only person I wanted to be with was Ty. He stopped over every day with Mom. I still had trouble looking at her. Even though I hated to admit it, I felt like I didn't love her anymore. I didn't feel much of anything for her. Except sorry. I felt sorry for her. Her leg was bandaged up, but she was walking around. She was back at school. Sometimes she talked about me going home with her, but she didn't push it too much. Ms. Collins said I could stay there as long as my mom said it was all right with her.

I finally went back to school. I sat in my classes, but it was hard to concentrate. The teacher would be halfway through the lesson, and I'd realize I hadn't heard a word. It was strange. I wouldn't just start to listen automatically. The words would slip down an invisible corridor in space and enter my head slowly, as if they were coming from a great distance. I'd have to hold my breath for a minute, then they'd slowly begin to make sense. First one word, then several, then I could hear sentences. But at first, when the words started coming, I could only hear one or two at a time.

I started training again. My muscles seemed to remember how to behave, even if I didn't. Once I got out on the track, I felt more alive. The wind lifted me up and took me to some other place where there were no demons and bogeymen.

Natonia stuck close by me most of the time. So did Esther, but they didn't ask any questions. Maybe they knew how I felt.

■ ■ ■

Almost two weeks after it happened, I thought maybe I would go home. I was packing my things, which my mother had brought over to Ms. Collins's for me. Ty came in and sat down on the bed Natonia and I slept in.

"He's back," Ty said.

I stopped packing.

"She didn't press charges."

I sat down on the bed.

"He says he's sorry."

I started taking my things back out of the suitcase.

"Don't do that," Ty said.

"I'm not coming home," I said. "It's not natural. A person doesn't shoot a bullet through another person and then come back in the house and live with them."

Ty didn't say anything. He just sort of collapsed onto the bed like he was thinking.

"I don't know," he said finally. "Maybe it *is* natural. It doesn't seem like it, but maybe it is. That's what happens in wars. People hate each other, and shoot each other. Lots of people die, then one side decides to surrender, and it's all over. Pretty soon everyone's friends again."

"Yeah, you told me that once, but it still doesn't make any sense," I said.

"Maybe not, but that's the way it is," Ty said. "World War II — guess who we were fighting."

I shrugged my shoulders.

"Germany and Japan."

I guess I kind of knew that, but I'd never thought much about it.

"Our TV is from Japan. A lot of the cars you see out there are from Japan or Germany. We're the best of friends with them now. And, of course, the Russians were fighting on our side, then after the war we hated them. Lots of people still do. I was watching this program the other day about Iraq, and you know what? When Iraq was fighting Iran, we gave Iraq all kinds of weapons to kill the Iranians, and then they used those weapons against us."

"How're you supposed to know who your friends and enemies are if they keep changing?"

"That's the point," Ty said.

"Still, it's different when it's in your own family."

"Maybe not. He wasn't always the enemy."

"I know."

"I talked to someone at school."

"Who?"

"Dr. Remley."

"About what?"

"About what happened."

"How come?"

"Mom wanted me to."

"And?"

"She was nice."

"You just talked?"

"Yeah. She asked me things. I told her I watched TV a lot, the news and stuff. She said I was right. Families fight like countries sometimes. Then they have to figure out how to make truces. She's pretty smart."

"You told her what he did?"

"She knew. At least I think she did, but she let me tell her when I was ready."

"Did you tell her everything?"

"No. I don't know everything."

I lay down on the bed. I was too tired to think.

"He sold the gun," Ty said. "He told me he did. He said he'd never have a gun in the house again."

I turned to look at Ty.

"Dad went to see Dr. Remley too. So did Mom."

A minute later, my mother called us from the living room. She'd been talking to Ms. Collins. Natonia was fixing dinner.

"You coming?" Ty asked.

I buried my head in the pillow.

"Please come home," he begged.

My body froze. I tried to remember what Ty said about wars and stuff, but all I could see was blood on the sidewalk. If I came home, I'd see it on the kitchen floor. It's too hard when you can't tell the difference between real life and your nightmares.

"I'll tell her you're not ready yet," Ty said.

I barely felt the bed move when he got up. It was as if he didn't have any flesh and bones that amounted to anything. For a moment I wondered if he'd really been there, or if I'd just imagined him. He was such a skinny little kid. I couldn't imagine him being a grown-up. But then again, in many ways he already was. He had to be.

22

Darren was giving everybody last-minute instructions. At least he was trying. But no one could sit still. So much electricity was coming out of our bodies that we got shocked when we touched each other. We were jumping up and down with excitement, hugging and laughing, scared and out of our minds with anticipation.

We were leaving tomorrow morning. Darren and Ms. Collins — who was going with us — would drive us to the airport, and we'd walk onto a plane and fly all the way to Pennsylvania. I'd never even been out of California. I wondered if there would be snow in Pennsylvania. I hoped so. I'd never seen snow, except in pictures.

"Okay, calm down," Darren said, but he was so excited, he could barely calm down himself. He was just pretending to be calm.

"You look great. You're ready for this meet. You're all going to jump and run your hearts out, and you're going to win every medal they have to offer. I want to plaster this wall with ribbons. I want to see a gold trophy on my desk next week."

"Yeah!" Everyone else shouted. I was wondering if they had all forgotten what happened in Los Angeles. Was I the only one who remembered what losers we'd been?

"Go home. Eat a good dinner. Do a few stretches tonight. And get a good night's sleep," Darren shouted above the clamor.

"Let's go," Natonia said.

Natonia hadn't had one of her moods in weeks. It wasn't that she was exactly bubbling over with affection, but she did give me a hug last night when we were talking about the trip.

"I gotta talk to Darren," I said urgently.

I walked over to him, but the whole time, I wasn't sure what it was I had to say.

Until I was standing right in front of him. Then I just said it. "I'm not going."

"Of course you are," he said.

"I can't."

"Kisha, we're counting on you."

"You'll do better without me."

"You know that's not true."

"It *is* true. You remember what happened in Los Angeles. I tripped over my own feet."

"People trip over their own feet all the time," Darren said, looking me straight in the eyes. "In one way or another."

"Not like me."

Darren stared at me for a minute like he thought I was saying something other than what I was saying. But I wasn't. I meant it just like I said it. I was bad news. I was selfish. I had too many things on my mind to concentrate on the track meet. I would screw up again. That's the way it was. Everyone in my family screwed up.

"Lots of people have setbacks in their lives. It's the winners who pick themselves up again and go on."

"I'm not a winner," I said. I could feel tears starting to slip out of my eyes. I wiped them away. One thing I wasn't was a crybaby. I never cried.

"Yes, you are," Darren said. He put his hands on my shoulders. "I'll see you tomorrow morning."

He turned and walked away. There was nothing more I could say. He might be disappointed when I didn't show up in the morning, but he couldn't say I didn't warn him.

On the other hand, maybe he'd be relieved.

I crossed the room and headed toward the door. Natonia was waiting for me. We walked back to Ms. Collins's place together, but I decided not to say anything more about the meet. It would just make her mad.

That night at dinner Ms. Collins asked, "You girls have everything ready for tomorrow?"

"I'm gonna pack right after dinner," Natonia said.

"Because we won't have time in the morning," Ms. Collins said. "We'll have to eat and run."

"I'm going to wear my new sweater," Natonia said. "No, maybe I'll pack it, and wear it when I get there. I don't want it to get mussed up."

"Underwear. You have enough clean underwear?"

"I think so," Natonia said.

It was like I wasn't even there. Neither of them asked me what I was planning to take. Maybe they knew I wasn't going.

"You know, Kisha," Ms. Collins said, like she could feel I was thinking about her. "I was wondering if I should mention this to you."

"Mention what?" I asked nervously.

"Your hair."

I slumped down into my chair. I knew my hair had

gotten to look even more freakish than usual. It was sticking up all over my head.

"I worked my way through school doing hair," Ms. Collins said. "I think I still remember a thing or two."

"Nothing you can do with this head," I moaned. "Believe me, I've tried."

"Get up," she said.

I got up and moved away from the table. She walked over to me, then she turned me around and around slowly. She went into the bathroom and came back with a towel, then she put the towel around my head like a turban. She studied my face.

"Good bones," she mumbled. "Great eyes. You can take it."

"You're not going to shave my head," I gasped as I reached up for the towel.

"You could get away with it," she said, and she laughed. "But that's not what I was thinking. Unless you're considering a music career."

"One bald-headed singer is enough," Natonia said.

I wondered if Sinead O'Connor had shaved her head one day when she just couldn't do anything with *her* hair.

"But short," Ms. Collins said. "Real short. That's the way to go."

I started to protest. I'd never really thought about

wearing my hair short. I'd spent my whole life trying to get it to grow out so it would look like my mother's. Even though I knew her hair was totally different from mine.

Then I decided, why not. My hair couldn't look much worse than it did now.

Ms. Collins ran her fingers though my hair and pulled it back this way and that. I liked the touch of her hands on my head. They were cool and sure. I gave myself up to her completely and followed her into the bathroom.

"Wash it," she commanded.

I obeyed, then I called to say I was ready.

Ms. Collins brought her piano stool in from the living room and motioned for me to sit down, then she put the towel around my shoulders and stared at me in the mirror.

Natonia squeezed into the bathroom, so she could watch the transformation.

I closed my eyes.

At one point I heard Natonia gasp, but I refused to open my eyes.

Every once in a while Ms. Collins muttered, "Ummm, ummm hummm."

After a while I drifted off, half forgetting where I was and what was happening to me.

Then Ms. Collins said, "Okay. Take a look."

Slowly, I opened my eyes. I reached up to my head. I looked like a totally different person. Was that me? My ugly hair was gone. Now there were tight curls half an inch long all over my head.

Well, I didn't look like the models in *Ebony* or *Essence,* with their long silky hair, but I looked — I looked like — me. Maybe this was the real me.

After I got over the shock, I thought I looked better than I'd ever looked. Instead of seeing a girl with ugly hair, I saw a girl with huge, round, brown eyes, long black lashes curling around them, staring back at me in the mirror.

"Black is beautiful," Ms. Collins said, and she sighed. "When I see the way you look, it reminds me of the way I looked in high school, and I have to say it again. Black *is* beautiful."

"You could be a model, Kisha," Natonia said. "You're built like one."

They both clapped for me when I got up to take a bow, which I did so they wouldn't see how emotional I felt.

"Nobody's going to recognize you tomorrow," Natonia said.

I froze. Somehow, I'd forgotten all about the track meet.

"I'm not going," I said.

Ms. Collins got busy cleaning up all the hair. I bent down to help her. No one said anything for a minute, but that didn't mean things weren't being communicated. It was like I'd dropped a bomb on them, and they were too stunned to react.

Natonia was taking short breaths, like it was too painful to reach way deep inside her lungs. Ms. Collins was taking long breaths, like she was trying to calm down. The heat coming off my body was spreading over the little bathroom. I was sweating. Now that I'd said it, I felt sick. And the worst part was that while I knew I had made the decision not to go, at this moment I couldn't remember why I had made that decision.

Finally, Natonia said, "You know what? I'm sick of your moods, girl. You think you're the only one in this world with troubles. Take a look around you, why don't you? If everyone just stopped living when something bad happened to them, half the people in this world would be dead. Hell, *all* the people at Whitman!"

She slammed out of the bathroom.

Ms. Collins didn't say a word. She just took the towel to shake it outside.

I stood in the middle of the room, feeling sorry for myself. No one understood me. No one.

When the phone rang, I jumped. The phone was in the kitchen, but it felt like it was ringing right in my head. I heard Ms. Collins answer it. Even though her voice was soft, I knew who she was talking to. I started walking toward the kitchen before she called my name.

"Hi, Mom," I said when I picked up the receiver.

"We just wanted to wish you luck," my mom said.

I knew I'd have to tell her. She'd be upset. Maybe she'd think I owed it to her to go. Suddenly, it dawned on me. I *did* owe her. After all, it was my fault she got shot. If she hadn't signed over her check to Darren, my father wouldn't have freaked out. I wanted to go for her sake. I wanted to rush home and cuddle up next to her on the couch, run my fingers up and down her arm, the way she likes me to. Feel her tickling my back with her long fingernails.

But I couldn't. My legs felt weak. I slid into a chair next to the kitchen table. I just couldn't.

"Here, Ty wants to say something, too," my mother said.

Ty got on the phone. "Wish I could be there tomorrow," he said. "I'll be thinking about you all day."

I started to cry.

"Mom wants to say something else."

"Dad would like to tell you good luck, too," she said.

"No," I yelled into the phone. "No. I'm not going. I changed my mind. I'm not going. I can't."

There was a long silence. I could hear my mother

breathing on the other end of the line. I sat there, my knuckles burning as I gripped the receiver.

"Kisha," my mom said after a long while. "I think I know how you feel."

"You don't know!" I shouted.

"Maybe not," she said softly. "But I do know one thing. I know what it's like to be shackled to a prison you can't get out of. I know how hard it is to break a cycle. I'm trying. I don't know if I'll make it. But *you* can. Go to the meet. That's your way out of here. Your ticket to a scholarship — a good education. Go. Run. *Run for your life!*"

23

I still don't understand how planes work. One minute we were sitting on the ground, and the next this big bird starts roaring and climbs into the sky. I mean, how does something that big just float in space? I don't know. There might be a scientific explanation, but it was magic to me.

"Hair's looking good, girl," Darren whispered as I walked past him toward the starting line. My engine started churning.

I stood there waiting for the first relay race to begin. I was trying to keep calm, the way Darren had told us to do, but that was a joke. My heart was speeding. The muscles of my legs were in spasm, and the race hadn't even begun.

I glanced at a girl a few feet away from me. It was the same girl who had made such nasty comments about us in Los Angeles.

I took a deep breath and raised my shoulders. I could see her glance at my hot pink outfit. I would have laughed out loud if I hadn't been so nervous. We were both second runners in this relay. Esther would start and hand the baton to me, then I would take it, run a quarter of a mile, and hand it to one of the twins. We'd practiced this a million times. Nothing could go wrong.

BANG! The starting gun went off.

Esther was racing toward me. I was ready to take off.

Just as Esther was about to place the baton in my hand the girl from the L.A. team knocked into me as she raced past. I dropped the baton. Stunned, I stood there for a second. Esther yelled, "Pick it up." On automatic now, I picked up the baton and sped around the track as fast as I could. But I couldn't make up the time we had lost.

We finished the race next to last.

Before the time was announced Darren ran up to the judges' stand, gesturing wildly. He was obviously upset. A few minutes later he walked back looking defeated, though he was trying not to show it.

"He said it was an accident," Darren said.

"The hell it was," Natonia hissed. "I was standing right there. That white girl deliberately knocked into Kisha."

I hadn't even considered that until Natonia said it. But as soon as she did, I knew it was true. That girl had deliberately knocked into me. And now that I thought about it, I remembered hearing her snicker as she ran past.

I almost started to cry. We were defeated before we had even had a chance to compete. The same thing would happen today that had happened in Los Angeles. Even the judge thought we were losers.

"That was one race," Darren said. "We have the rest of the day to prove ourselves."

"And we will, too!" Natonia yelled.

She looked over at the girl from L.A. and sneered at her. I had never seen such anger in my life. To tell the truth, it scared me a little, even though it wasn't aimed at me.

"When I'm mad, watch out," Natonia said as she walked over to the starting line for the 100-meter individual event.

Natonia stood taller than any of the other girls competing. Before she bent into running position, she looked over at me, her jaw clenched, fire in her eyes, ready to kick the butt of anyone who got in her way. No one would dare knock into Natonia.

BANG! They were off.

We screamed and cried, running along with Natonia in our minds and hearts. My muscles ached, straining to push her along to victory.

They dashed toward the finish. It was so close. Four girls were running neck and neck. I closed my eyes. I couldn't look.

Then it was all over. Everyone was screaming.

I opened my eyes. Natonia was sobbing.

My heart sank. Natonia was our best bet for a medal.

I didn't know what to do. What could I say?

I walked over to her. "We've still got the rest of the day," I said, but the words didn't have much meaning for me, and probably not for her, either.

She couldn't stop crying.

Finally, the judge was announcing the times over the P.A. "In third place Alma Jean McAllister, running — "

Natonia let out a wail.

"In second place Natonia Washington, running — "

I screamed so loud I almost lost my voice. Second place! Second place in a national meet! This was incredible.

Natonia was still sobbing.

"Why are you crying?" I screamed. "You won second!"

"Because I'm so happy," she said between her sobs.

That was all it took. One win, and we were really there, in our heads as well as our bodies.

We took second and third in the 200-meter race. First and third in the long jump, and second and third in the 400-meter race. If nothing else, we had stamina.

The rain was falling on us, but we didn't care. Let it come. Nothing could stand in our way now.

We lined up for the last event of the day. The 800-meter race. We were all participating. But we weren't competing against each other. We were competing against every other team. It didn't matter who won what. What mattered was that we were a team.

BANG! We were off. The wind and rain swept me off my feet as I ran against them. *I'm flying,* I thought as I hurtled through space, passing runner after runner. *Now* I know how a plane works! I kept it up, pacing myself, feeling lightheaded and lighthearted. Now there was no one else running. It was just me and the wind and rain taking me someplace I'd never been. Then there wasn't any me anymore, just a hot pink bird flying past the finish line. First.

I was dazed as the judge announced the winners: Esther Jones, third; Jennifer Dunne, second; Kisha Carter, first place.

Our team had taken first, second, and third place. Not only that, we had broken the national record for the 800-meter race.

The rain was still coming down, but it was only a

drizzle now. We ran toward the platform to receive our medals. All of us. Because all of us had won. I was about to skirt a huge puddle when I noticed Ms. L.A. I stepped hard into the puddle, splashing mud all over her fancy track suit.

"Ooops, an accident," I yelled to her. Then I smiled and ran to catch up with my team.

The girls who went back to the hotel were different from the ones who had boarded the plane yesterday. We all felt it.

There was a rush for the showers, the usual giggling and talking, the screaming and carrying on, but it was more subdued.

We all got dressed and studied our images in the mirror.

"I don't know what it is," Malika said, "but you look different. You look so pretty."

I could feel my face heating up.

"It's her haircut," Shanika said. "It looks great."

"Yeah, you're right. It's the haircut."

I smiled. The haircut helped, but I knew that's not what it really was.

■ ■ ■

This time you couldn't have pulled us away from the awards banquet. We stood there and smiled and smiled until our lips hurt, and then we smiled some more.

Everyone came up to congratulate us afterward. Well, not everyone. But most people. We made all kinds of new friends. Out of the corner of my eye I saw a group of white girls come over to Jennifer. I couldn't hear exactly what they were saying, but they seemed to be inviting her to come over to their table and sit with them.

She started fidgeting, like she did sometimes when she was uncomfortable, and she shook her head, no.

Then she walked over to where I was standing and stood next to me.

"We won," she whispered.

"Yeah," I said. "We did."

Afterward, back at the hotel, Darren and Ms. Collins sat us down in a circle. We were all still congratulating ourselves on being the big winners of the day.

"Any of you on drugs?" Darren asked.

He looked at each one of us individually.

"No!" we all shouted.

"Anyone pregnant?" he asked.

"All of us," we said.

214

Darren about dropped dead on the spot. We laughed our heads off.

"Anyone getting less than a C in school?"

"Just in math," Alisha said.

"You're right," Darren said. "You *are* winners."

"And so are you," we shouted back at him.

24

When we got back to Oakland, we marched off the plane, our shoulders straight and our heads high. Then we walked right through that airport like we'd done it dozens of times before.

A porter came over to Darren and asked him who he was and why he was traveling with such a fine-looking group of girls.

Darren told him, and he added that we were all in training for the Olympics.

At first we laughed, but then I thought—why not?

The porter said, "I like what you're doing, my friend. Hold on a second."

He whipped out his checkbook and wrote Darren a check.

"I'm sure your team will need some traveling money for future tournaments."

Darren looked at the check, and his eyes about popped out of his head.

"I can't take this from you," he cried.

"Looks can be deceiving," the porter said. He winked at Darren. "I run this concession. I'm just filling in for someone today."

He scribbled something on a piece of paper and handed it to Darren. "Here's my address. Keep me posted. And let me know if you need anything. I have a few friends, too."

He waved to us and walked on. "See you at the Olympics," he called as he disappeared into the crowd.

Darren kissed the check and put it in his pocket. "Kisha, Natonia, and Esther go with Ms. Collins," he said. "I'll take the kids who live at Whitman in my car."

"I live at Whitman," I said softly.

Both Natonia and Darren looked at me for a moment, but neither of them said anything.

"Slipped my mind," Darren said. "Come on. Let's go home."